How to Go Through
HELL

How to Go Through

HELL

Richard Jarzynka

BALBOA.
PRESS

A DIVISION OF HAY HOUSE

Balboa Press books may be ordered through booksellers or by contacting:

Balboa Press
A Division of Hay House
1663 Liberty Drive
Bloomington, IN 47403
www.balboapress.com
1 (877) 407-4847

Because of the dynamic nature of the Internet, any web addresses or links contained in this book may have changed since publication and may no longer be valid. The views expressed in this work are solely those of the author and do not necessarily reflect the views of the publisher, and the publisher hereby disclaims any responsibility for them.

The author of this book does not dispense medical advice or prescribe the use of any technique as a form of treatment for physical, emotional, or medical problems without the advice of a physician, either directly or indirectly. The intent of the author is only to offer information of a general nature to help you in your quest for emotional and spiritual well-being. In the event you use any of the information in this book for yourself, which is your constitutional right, the author and the publisher assume no responsibility for your actions.

Any people depicted in stock imagery provided by Thinkstock are models, and such images are being used for illustrative purposes only. Certain stock imagery © Thinkstock.

Print information available on the last page.

All Scripture quotes are taken from "Good News Bible: Today's English Version." American Bible Society (1976)

ISBN: 978-1-5043-4817-1 (sc)
ISBN: 978-1-5043-4818-8 (e)

Balboa Press rev. date: 1/19/2016

DAY ONE

BANG!

Hallelujah Livingstone's first day in this place was about to begin; and he figured his only way out was to be sent someplace worse.

Bang!

"A-a-a-w-w," Hallelujah groaned, at 6:03am, and rolled his 6-foot-6-inch frame over on the two-inch thick slab of rubber that covered his metal-framed cot.

Bang! Bang!

"A-a-a-w-1! . . . What in the blazes is that?!"

The guards, aides, nurses, counselors, and blood-hounds were arriving for duty and letting the heavy, double-metal doors slam behind them, giving an electric jump-start to any sleeping soul within fifty feet of the seventh floor's entrance.

And Hallelujah, who was known by most as "Stone," now hated to wake up – at any time of day, in any way. It meant that his brain – or something - would start up again with all of that *"You're no good . . . Look at the mess you've made of yourself . . . you're life – everybody's life . . . You never cared about anybody but yourself."*

And he wouldn't be able to shut it off for the next 15 hours – not for a second.

"You evil trash," it started. And Stone cringed in pain.

"Good morning, Mr. Livingstone!" a cheerful, bright and gangly young man, of no more than 20 years, smiled from Stone's doorway. "Breakfast is in the Community Room."

"Look at that!" Stone's brain attacked, sounding like something other than his brain. *"That kid has a real job. A responsible job . . . And here you are – 26 years old and still can't support your pitiful self. You oughtta be ashamed."*

Stone glanced at the young man – an aide on this floor – and quickly noticed his ring.

"How do like that?!" mocked Stone's miserable brain – or something. *"That kid is married . . . and you've never kept a woman for more than two dates . . . Because . . . you just don't . . . CARE . . . about anybody! . . . Do you, sociopath?!"*

Stone grabbed his head and pushed his hands frantically, over and over, through his dark, shoulder-length, red hair.

"No!" he groaned. "No, blast it," but he believed what that sound in his brain was telling him.

"Easy, Mr. Livingstone," the young aide comforted. "It's not the best breakfast in the world, but it's not *that* bad."

Stone twitched and jerked his head to the left. His eyes darted. His right hand went frantically through his hair again. "I'm sorry," he said to the aide, "I wasn't yelling at you."

Stone didn't want breakfast, but the life that had once flamed inside of him was in no mood to break the rules. The fire wasn't extinguished, but it was down to a few smoldering embers. He stumbled raggedly to the community room and ate - slowly – trying to distract himself, hardly tasting the hash of oatmeal, cup of applesauce, and bacon.

And 20 egg-dreary minutes later, Stone stumbled back to his room, dropped to his bed, and thunder exploded in his doorway, roaring, "Hal— a-a—L-u-u-u— yah!! Livingstone!!!" It boomed

Wildman. It beamed and howled and soared. "My goodness! 'Hallelujah Livingstone.'What a name that is!" the obvious lunatic yelled. And Stone jumped to his feet with a thousand volts, unable to say a word.

"Ezra Eliot Loleko," the power-plant of madness blasted away to Stone; with a big, wild, barrel-lunged laugh. "That's _my_ name!"

Everything about this man blazed out loud. He was blowing up all over the place. All "Yes! Yes! Yes!" He filled the doorway with neon and looked 7-feet tall in Stone's eyes, but he was actually the exact same 6'6" as Stone.

"Ezra Eliot Loleko," the giant roared. "How in the world did I get a name like that? . . . Well, my ma was a part-time English professor," he sped on, answering his own question, "and my old man was a joker, who hated school, but ended up teaching because it gave him all the time in the world to do what he really loved – howlin' out loud in a country-punk band."

"Huh?" Stone grunted a nearly-panicked laugh."

"Yes! Yes!" Ezra raved. "My ma was an English professor and my dad sang – if you could call it that – in a country-punk band," he rambled and raged. "Sounded like a screaming coyote, but I loved it . . . So, I ended up getting named after three dead poets."

"Ezra Pound and T.S. Eliot," Stone quickly responded, much to Ezra's delight," And, uh-umm—"

"e.e cummings! – Ezra Eliot, e.e. - Nuts, ain't it?" Loleko cackled.

"W-what are you?" Stone shakily managed to ask, overwhelmed by the raging ball of fire.

"H-a-a-a!" Ezra boomed with glee. "I'm just like you, Brother Livingstone!"

Ezra was locked up in this place just like Stone, but he was the freest man Stone had ever seen. The truth is; he wasn't locked up at all. He couldn't be locked up . . . And Stone would have been locked up even if he was free to roam the most wide open prairie in the land.

3

But Ezra Eliot Loleko was, indeed, a lot like Hallelujah Livingstone.

They both stood 6'6" and were 225 pounds of brick, mortar, and muscle. Together, they could have torn the place apart. But there wasn't much fight left in Stone and Ezra wouldn't lay his hand on another — and he would have no other lay a hand on him — but there weren't many so inclined.

The two men were both athletes, though Ezra had rarely played an organized sport, while Stone had been a right-handed relief pitcher, including one year on a baseball scholarship to Vanderbilt University — known to some as "the Harvard of the South." It seemed like another lifetime. It was another lifetime.

Stone had a 93 mile per hour sinking fastball that missed as many bats as Stone did classes. And he wasn't all that interested in going to class.

That, however, does not mean that Stone was some kind of an idiot. One does not get to Vanderbilt University without brains — even on an athletic scholarship. But Stone's mind — or something — was already attacking him in that freshman year at Vanderbilt and he feared treatment.

Stone didn't want medication — or any kind of therapy - while he was pitching in college. He rightly figured that it would mess with his brain. And he didn't want anyone to know how much his brain needed to be messed with — especially his coaches. So, he looked forward to stopping the lightning in his head by getting full-blown drunk on Thursday nights in the sewer-like basement of some fraternity — any fraternity.

And that caused him to miss class all day Friday. Every Friday. But, somehow, he managed to pitch one or two innings of all three weekend games. And as soon as the Sunday games ended, he would find a bar far enough into the woods of suburban Nashville to be free from any thorn-in-the-keester, college kids. And get drunk — again.

Stone's grades weren't good, but his 2.5 QPA was better than one would expect, given the number of classes he missed. However, they weren't quite good enough to keep a scholarship at a top-notch academic institution like Vanderbilt. So, Stone spent his last three years at a Division II school near his home in Wheeling, West Virginia. And made loans to pay his tuition.

With his undiagnosed brain raging, Stone needed the support of being close to his home, his family, and his high school friends. It all helped to get him through school, perform on the baseball field – and limit his drinking. But the school loans were now a heavy burden. He was close to defaulting and he beat himself daily for losing the scholarship to Vanderbilt.

Even at an obscure Division II school, Stone's sinking fastball was good enough to get him noticed by pro scouts. And the bulk he put on between age 18 and age 21 had taken the velocity on his pitches from 93 mph to 95.3. That may not sound like much of an increase, but it was enough to get him drafted into professional baseball by the Minnesota Twins in the 22nd round.

Most of the best college players are drafted into pro baseball after their junior season. Stone wasn't considered to be one of the best – or even in the second tier, so he had to wait until he finished his senior season; and very few players who are passed over for the first 21 rounds of the draft ever get anywhere close to the major leagues. But Stone's hard-sinking fastball and the sweeping slider he added in his senior year gave him a chance.

"You don't seem at all like me, Mr. Loleko," Stone replied to Ezra's incongruent answer to his "What are you?" question.

"We're the tallest, strongest, most athletic men in this whole joint," Ezra laughed.

"Probably, yeah . . . I guess," Stone said, almost apologetically.

"And . . . more importantly, Mr. Livingstone . . . we're Brothers-in-Madness! I'm just like you!" Ezra howled with his eyes flashing bright turquoise and rolling wildly around their sockets – for exactly the intended effect.

"Your madness doesn't seem much like mine," Stone lamented, sounding oddly envious.

"N-a-a-h," Ezra grinned. "Yours is just all bound up – and mine got uncranked a long time ago."

Stone just stared. There was a force-field around Ezra that drew him in, but Ezra's uncranked madness was more than he could handle or understand.

"How did you get in here?" Ezra asked.

"That's a long story – and it's probably been a long time comin'. Feels like I've been headed here all my life."

"Gimme the condensed version."

"I'm no rippin' good," Stone snapped. "And I'm getting what I deserve."

"I won't argue with you on that one," Ezra smiled gently – and sincerely – looking straight into Stone's eyes.

That stunned Stone. Everyone else had been vehemently trying to convince him that he was a kind, loving, gem of a man, who shouldn't be suffering such a tormenting, panicked, and delusional depression.

"I'm no rippin' good," Stone said again – and hesitated. He knew that the rest of what he had to say would sound crazy – and even in his current residence, he didn't want to sound _that_ crazy . . .

Ezra waited.

"I'm evil," Stone barked at himself, still holding back on the full, nonsensical nightmare of what he was thinking. "I've never been any good . . . never cared about anything but myself."

"Well, then, it seems perfectly natural . . . that you would be going through hell," Ezra said firmly, in a voice filled with manly concern.

"My brain never stops slamming me with every miserable thing I've ever done. Every failure. Every person I've ever hurt. Every blarin' failure . . . And it's constant . . . And it won't ever end."

Ezra now looked even more directly at Stone and his voice went deep and strong. "I know what you need to do to get through this," he insisted.

"There ain't no getting through this," Stone said lowly and firmly, looking at the floor to his right.

"It's never too late!" Ezra demanded. "Not as long as you're on the sunny-side of the dirt."

Stone jerked his head suddenly to the left and back to the right. *"Sunny-side?! Ha!"* That thing that sounded like his brain was on the attack again. *"There ain't no help for you,"* it knifed. *"This is it, you no good leech! It's over . . . And it's only going to get worse."*

Stone wasn't so sure that he was still on "the sunny-side of the dirt." He believed that he had completely given up. He had planned to commit suicide the night before he entered the hospital, but he couldn't go through with it. Couldn't even take the first step of his plan.

And Stone had not come to the hospital hoping to "get better." Or even "get through this." He just wanted to put his family out of his misery. And he hoped that, maybe, the doctors would eventually give up, too. That they would realize he was beyond help and just drug him safely into numb oblivion.

So, when Ezra said that he knew what Stone needed to do to "get through this," Stone figured it was a madman's load of bunk." . . . But Ezra was too much to resist – and there was still a flicker of something in Stone that wanted, hopelessly, to believe.

DAY TWO

IT WAS A DEVILISH WAY TO WAKE UP.

Lights flashing blue and red like a fire truck blasting through the door. A burly-fat, loud man with a large, growling head barreled into the room. Pushing a strange, metal machine, he barked something unintelligible and charged toward the side of Stone's bed.

"What's this?" Stone snapped, three-quarters unconscious.

And the large-headed barbarian grabbed Stone's right wrist and – only then – groused, "Blood work," as the needle hit the vein at the crux of Stone's elbow.

Just a few months earlier, that would have sent big-head sprawling at the end of Stone's hard left fist. But there wasn't nearly that much fight left in him now. He lay back, not wanting to make waves. And it started. *"What did you expect ? . . . There ain't no rest for the wicked."*

Stone rolled over as the blood-hound and his metal contraption left the room. And zap! He jumped as if he had been poked in the head with a hot wire. He snapped violently back-and-forth in bed, as the words struck again, *"No rest for the wicked, you evil monster! Hell is too good for you."*

And so began Stone's second day locked in the nuthouse.

It was 6:30am and the strange sounds of Stone's brain were already on the attack. And Stone knew it was useless. There would, indeed, be *no rest* for the next 14 hours – when he would get his longed-for trip into cold non-consciousness; from an unnamed drug that knocked him into dreamless sleep . . . But he tried anyway. He needed to escape. He grabbed his head with both arms and buried it in a pillow, but the electricity instantly hit his brain with another word – and he went thrashing again.

And so it went for the next hour – until the cheerful, bright and gangly, young man smiled, again, from the doorway, and sang, "Good morning, Mr. Livingstone . . . Breakfast is in the Community Room."

Stone had never liked eggs and he had no appetite for much of anything, but he needed a distraction, so he poked at the yellow lumps and put them to his mouth without tasting them.

"Is this decaf?" Stone asked about the coffee.

"Yeah," replied and aide, in a way that said he wasn't sure.

Stone left it alone. He wasn't going to drink anything that might wake him up any more than necessary.

Again – as soon as he got back to his room, he was zapped upright by the blare of "Hal – u-h-h – Loooo – yah Livingstone!"

Ezra's voice boomed and roared merrily from the doorway. And Stone was, somehow, relieved to see him. There was something about the mad, power-plant of a giant that brought him something almost like brief moments of peace.

"Well, you've had a full day to think about it," Ezra pronounced.

"Yeah, what?"

"Are you ready to work your way through this?" Ezra asked and reminded.

"Oh, yeah, that . . . You've got the secret for how to fix me." Stone smirked – and hoped at the same time.

"Yes. Yes, I do . . . But I'm not giving it to you unless you commit to doing it."

"You want me to commit to doing something _before_ you tell me what it is that I'm going to doing?" Stone incredulously objected.

"That's right."

"That's wrong," Stone shot back.

"It ain't gonna kill ya; this plan I've got," said Ezra. "It ain't no sin – or even a crime. And . . . given the shape your mind is in . . . what have you really got to lose?"

"Yeah, I burned up good, but I'm not an idiot. I'm not making any promises without knowing what I'm getting into first."

Ezra shrugged, cocking his head to the left. "I'm asking you to trust me."

"I don't," Stone firmly stated. But he knew that everything about Ezra said that he could.

"I'm sure that you can handle it," Ezra smiled coyly, - almost encouragingly . . . "But if you don't have that kind of confidence, I'm not going to try to force it on you."

Stone heard the challenge in that statement and it almost hacked him off enough to stand up to it; but he feared not taking Ezra up on his offer to show him the way out of this hell. It was probably nothing more than the nonsense of a nuthouse vigilante, but nothing else was working. And Ezra's comment that he didn't really have anything to lose hit home with Stone.

Whatever Ezra's plan was, Stone thought, it certainly did seem to be working for him. The man was six-and-a-half feet of unbridled, muscular joy. He grinned and cackled – he bounced and beamed and boomed with enthusiasm. He laughed. Easily, loudly – and often. He seemed to be everything that Stone was not – and wished he could be. But Ezra had said that they were "just alike" – Brothers-in-Madness. That the only difference was that Ezra's madness had "uncranked" a long time ago, but Stone's was still all bound up – constipating his mind, soul, and spirit. Just like the medications were doing to his body.

"This plan," Stone thought, "maybe that's what got him _uncranked_."

Long ago, Stone had moments of that kind of uncranked, joyful cackling, booming, beaming madness. But those brief, but intense, moments were quickly followed with whispers - *"You're no good, you selfish freak"* - and all the sinister nagging that sent him crashing, ranting, and going dark for days on end.

Stone wanted the light that glowed in – and from – Ezra. He wanted to believe that the madman knew what he was talking about. He wanted to believe . . . but he was so far gone.

Ezra pierced Stone's ruminations with an affirmation of everything Stone had been thinking.

"Maybe you don't trust me," Ezra charged. "Maybe you shouldn't . We've only just met and all you know about me is that I'm a ball-of-fire locked up in a nuthouse. Most would call you crazy for trusting me."

"You got that right," Stone snapped and laughed.

"So, I'm asking you to take a leap of faith."

"Faith?!" Stone yelped. "You just gave me all the reasons why I don't know that I can trust you."

"Faith ain't knowin'," Ezra shot back firmly – suddenly sober. "Faith is doubting and deciding to believe, anyway, in spite of the fact that you don't *know* – <u>can't</u> know. It's lookin' at all your doubts . . . all your good reasons for doubting –and going ahead, anyway, because you believe there might be something good that's worth the chance. It's courage. It's faith. The kind of faith it takes to make a commitment – and keep it."

"Yeah. Why not just tell me the plan?" Stone demanded, tempted to jump in, but needing more.

"Because I want to know that you're the kind of man who can make a commitment," Ezra challenged, when he could have gone easy. "Because I want <u>*you*</u> to know that you're the kind of man who can *keep* a commitment."

"You're a crazy-happy, all-excited-with-life . . . tough buzzard," Stone snapped, almost playfully.

"That's me!" Ezra hooted. "Maybe, you can be one, too."

"Maybe . . . Ahh, blast it," Stone shook his head in disbelief at what he was about to say. "I'll do it . . . Whatever you're screwball plan is . . . What's the worst that can happen?"

"Good question . . . They could let you outta here and you'd have to deal with the rest of the world."

"No thanks . . . There's a lotta nuts out there," Stone chuckled softly, shaking his head at the thought of what he might be getting himself into.

"Okay, here's the deal," Ezra smiled, pulling a small booklet out of his pocket, but not giving it to Stone.

"You've got it all written out for me?"

"You read one page of this booklet, first thing in the morning. You read the same page in the afternoon. And you read it again, right before you go to bed."

"That's it?"

"It's not as easy as you think."

"What's the hard part?"

Ezra smiled. "You have to think about it."

"I think a lot."

"This is gonna be different."

Stone cocked his head, smiled, and shrugged. "I guess I need *'different'*."

"You're gonna think about this. And, without realizing it, you're going to start to dwell on it – or, rather, _dwell-with_ it. And, as you _dwell-with_ it, a line or two – maybe three – is going to stand out to you."

"You're sure about that, huh," Stone smirked, a little miffed at the way Ezra had presumed to know what would take place in his mind.

But Ezra wasn't playing.

"Remember those lines," Ezra firmly instructed. "Fix them in your mind."

"I will," Stone responded, matching the urgency in Ezra's tone

"Those lines that stand out to you," Ezra reiterated. "This matters . . . Say them in your own words."

"Why?"

"Say them in your own words," Ezra repeated, "So, you'll understand them and remember them . . . and . . ." Ezra stopped and slightly shook his head.

"And what?" Stone pressed.

"You don't need to know that."

"I *want* to know it," Stone insisted.

"Not now."

"You're holding something back on me, but you want me to commit to doing this?"

"You already committed to doing this." Ezra smiled and almost winked.

"You said, 'pick out a verse that hits home with me . . . say it in my own words –"

"Yes. So, you'll really understand it –"

"And remember it," Stone interrupted .

"Right. Can we move on now?"

"No," Stone snapped. "You said there is something more I need to do with those verses – and if you want to move on, you're going to tell me what that is."

"You don't need to know that," Ezra softly insisted. "It will happen before you know it, without even trying – when the verses hit home and you dwell-with them, say them in your own words, and remember them . . . understand them."

"No it won't," Stone snapped again, growing more impatient with Ezra's tactic.

But Ezra wasn't going to be moved so easily.

"I'm telling you it will," he said. "I've seen it happen many times."

"It ain't happenin' like that with Hallelujah Livingstone!"

"O-o-h! Hallelujah is different than everybody else."

"Could be," Hallelujah defiantly smiled. "I don't know. But Hallelujah ain't doin' any of it, unless you tell him all of it."

"I like that."

"What? Whaddaya like?" Stone asked, surprised – and still defiant.

"You ain't had the nerve to talk like that to somebody in a long time . . . have you?"

Stone lowered his head and frowned himself right back into timidity . . . But Ezra Eliot Loleko wouldn't let him stay there.

"You still got it in you, Hallelujah."

"What?" Stone mumbled.

"Fight! . . . Fire. A spirit that wants to break out of hell and live . . . Now stand up!"

Stone could not resist the strange power bursting out of Ezra Eliot Loleko. And he snapped to his feet without thinking.

"And make it a part of you!" Ezra roared.

"Make what a part of me?" Stone asked, now foggily puzzled with all of Ezra's misdirection.

"Pick out a line that hits home with you. Dwell-with it. Say it in your own words so you'll understand it and remember it . . . And make it . . . a part of you," Ezra said gently, strongly . . . with the calm conviction of a man.

That evening, after the med window call and taking his Depakote, Paxil, Seroquel and a sleeping pill without a name, Hallelujah collapsed onto his metal cot with its two-inch thick "mattress." He craved that sleeping pill. It shut down his brain – and all day long his brain had raged with *"You're no good . . . "This place is too good for you . . . You selfish fraud, you never loved anybody, never cared about anybody - but yourself . . . You coward momma's boy . . . Lived your whole life in fear . . . You had it made – and now look at you"* and Stone's rock-solid belief that there was no way out.

Hallelujah glanced at the small, metal end-table bolted to the floor beside his bed. His admission papers, patients' bill of rights, treatment plan, and consent forms were crumbled and strewn across it. And atop of that mess, about which he could not care less, sat the booklet which Ezra had given him and he had agreed to read.

Stone frowned. He didn't hold out much hope for that little booklet, but he had agreed – or "committed" – to reading for just one day. And Ezra – there was something about him that tempted Stone to have a small grain of hope . . . So, why not? . . . What, indeed, did he have to lose?

Hallelujah briefly – just for a second – considered opening the booklet. But Ezra had admonished him not to read it until morning and to only read one page per day.

Stone had no trouble rolling over and forgetting the plan, the booklet, and Ezra. He craved the shutting down of his brain.

The good thing about the nameless pill was that it put him out as soon as his head hit the Styrofoam pad that didn't quite pass for a pillow. The bad thing about the pill was that it knocked him out so thoroughly loaded that the next eight hours passed like five minutes. And it kept him from dreaming – or maybe just remembering – but not tonight.

This night, Stone dreamed of a lean man, with the rugged features of a middle-aged face, standing boldly at the top of a skyscraper. And the very next picture in his mind was a child – a boy, maybe seven years old – slowly circling his bicycle around the man lying face-down on the sidewalk.

Stone didn't know whether he was the child or the man. Or both.

DAY THREE

STONE FINALLY RAISED HIS 6-FOOT-6-INCH FRAME UP. HE hated having to do it. It would start his mind racing non-stop for the next 16 hours. But once the doors started banging, it was useless. And the nurses and their assistants wouldn't let him just lie there for long. Every few minutes, somebody would be by to nag him out of his cherished oblivion. He knew the routine and understood it.

The nurses, counselors, doctors, and aides knew that lying in bed all day was no therapy for depression. In fact, it was a prescription for how to get depressed. But Stone wasn't buying any of it. He was beyond therapy – psycho, chemo, electro, and otherwise.

He slumped to the edge of his bed and sat there, head down, for a full sixty seconds. When he finally heaved himself to his feet, his vision went dark and he swayed like an aging reed in an autumn wind. And, after a rocky, dazed moment, he steadied himself and headed – out of stupored routine – for the bathroom. But he was stopped dead in his tracks. A voice that didn't sound like the others in his head whispered firmly, *"You said that you were going to read as soon as you woke up."*

"Aw, gimme a blasted break!" Stone griped out loud, halfway to the toilet. "Can't I even take a – Aw! Can't even do *this* in peace?!"

"You can still be a man of your word," the voice said firmly, yet somehow gently, at the same time. *"You made a commitment."*

Stone picked up the booklet and sat in the pale blue, metal chair that was bolted to the floor in the corner of the room – just like the pale blue, metal end-table beside his bed. And he began to read.

"When you pray-- "[1]

Stone twitched violently and cringed. "No," he whispered and growled, "He doesn't get it!"

It wasn't that Stone didn't believe in God. Indeed, he believed now more than ever. But it was too late. He was under the wrath of God and there was no getting out from under it. He deserved every bit of God's anger, he told himself.

"You turned your back on God," another voice blasted and accused. *"It is finished, for you . . . God isn't letting you back . . . This little booklet 'plan' was sent to torture you."*

Stone clenched his fists and buried his head in his arms. The booklet fell to the floor. He groaned from his belly, hoarsely up through his aching chest and throat – for a long time. Lowly, hurting, despairing - but still worried that somebody might hear – and laugh.

He couldn't speak, couldn't think. He groaned. And kept groaning.

"Keep your commitment," the strange, new, firm but gentle voice in his brain whispered; sounding like something outside of his mind. *"Keep your commitment. That's all that matters, right now, and what have you got to lose? . . . Read that passage . . . Read it again this afternoon . . . Talk with Ezra about it and read again before you go to bed."*

He was locked in a living psych ward hell. Reading the words Ezra left for him might hurt, but he was going to hurt – bad – anyway. And Ezra had a hope for him that felt real – and, somewhere, deep inside, Hallelujah Livingstone wanted desperately to hope.

He picked the booklet off the floor and opened back to the first page.

"When you pray . . . do not use a lot of meaningless words, as the pagans do, who think that God will hear them because their prayers are long. Do not be like them. Your Father already knows what you need before you ask him."[2]

At noon, Stone forced himself to finish half a hamburger and a bowl of coleslaw during the Community Room lunch. At 2:45, he met with Ezra.

"I read it," Stone said, "but it can't work."

"It can't work," Ezra repeated, intentionally choosing not to challenge Stone's assertion.

Stone shook his head – hard – and bit his lip.

"What did it say?"

"It's good. It's holy . . . It's real. But it can't work . . . Not for me." Stone repeated.

"Not for you," Ezra gave the words back to Stone.

Stone gazed glassy-eyed at the floor, as at nothing.

"You're holding something back," Ezra smiled, but spoke firmly.

"Something? . . ." Stone lifted his voice, almost playfully. "There's a lot I haven't said. We just met."

"True . . . But there is something that you have been trying to tell me . . . and haven't yet been able."

Stone stared.

Ezra didn't say a word.

"What makes you think you know what is going on in my head?" Stone jabbed, with more than a hint of confrontation.

"You say you're evil. You say that you're mind is beating you up . . . and that you're getting what you deserve---"

"Yeah," Stone interrupted, only halfway trying to keep Ezra from pushing.

"And then you clench your teeth and grind your lips into a hard frown . . . forcing your next words to stay in your mouth." Ezra said firmly, looking directly into Stone's eyes.

And Stone clenched his teeth and frowned – hard.

"There it is again," Ezra challenged. "It's right there . . . trying to burst out."

Stone said nothing.

"I won't ask you to tell me what it is that you're holding back. That's your business." Ezra reassured, "But I will ask what it is that's keeping you from telling me."

And Stone felt a little more comfortable with the matter. "It's too crazy," he said, causing Ezra to smile.

"Yeah, I know," Stone went on, through tight lips. "But even for this place, it's too crazy."

"Yeah," Ezra grinned, "but I don't belong to this place."

"Why'd ya start any of this with me?" Stone cracked. "You know I'm too far gone . . . So why'd ya gimme this plan – this blasted idea that I can get through this . . . this . . ."

"This what?" Ezra pounced.

Stone frowned, but it wasn't quite as hard . . . and his teeth weren't clenched.

"What are you going through, Stone?" Ezra said gently, in a way that meant serious business.

"I _am_ gone," Stone growled, the words bursting through his lips. "I'm too _far_ gone!" he blasted.

"We've been through that already," Ezra said, unfazed. "You agreed that you can't _know_ that you're too far gone."

Stone stared past Ezra, frowning and shaking his head.

"You _can't_ know," Ezra demanded. "You can't _know_ that it's too late for you," he growled. "You can't _know_ that you don't still have a real chance," he kept pushing.

"Blast it, man!" Stone growled back.

"Yeah! Blast it . . . Take a blasted chance . . . You're a man!" Ezra challenged. "Take a blasted chance."

"It's hell! You lunatic!" Stone barked and growled and snapped.

"Yeah! . . . I know! . . . You're going through hell."

"No!" Stone roared with such ferocity that it caused even the 6-foot-6-inch power-plant of Ezra Eliot Loleko to pull back.

"Wow," Ezra said, impressed with Stone's passion. "So, tell me . . . If you're not going through hell, what is it?"

"It IS hell. It's not a way of saying, 'I'm going through a bad time' . . . It's not a metaphor."

"Its very real, Hallelujah," Ezra affirmed, in a knowing way that surprised – and strangely calmed - Stone. "It's deadly real," he continued, "even if it is a metaphor."

"You're not getting it."

"I think I am."

"Not possible," Stone demanded.

"You're not going through hell like some people say they are in pain. You're not saying, 'I'm going through hell,' meaning that you're in the middle of the worst time of your life . . ."

Stone listened hard . . . was it possible that Ezra . . . *could* . . . understand what anybody in his right mind would call impossible?

"This isn't just a bad, bad, painful time," Ezra lowly breathed. "This isn't a metaphor . . . for you, Stone . . . You believe that you are in Hell."

Stone dropped his head and lowered his eyes. His face went limp. Slowly, he looked back at Ezra . . . And Ezra continued.

"You believe, don't' you . . . that you are _literally_ in Hell."

"How could you know that?" Stone asked, bewildered.

Ezra slightly, and knowingly, smiled.

Stone looked back blankly. Stunned.

Ezra spoke gently. "Tell me about it, Stone."

"I couldn't take it anymore. My brain beating me constantly. Torturing me with everything I ever screwed up. Every evil thing I ever did. I couldn't function. I couldn't break out of it. It just kept beating . . . beating at me, beating at my brain – in my brain . . . And it was all true. I was evil . . . Am . . . It was destroying me. And it wasn't just me . . . It was tearing my family apart. Emotionally . . . destroying my parents . . ."

"It was destroying you," Ezra simply repeated. "Tearing your family apart. . . . Destroying your parents . . . Emotionally."

"And it wasn't ever going to end," Stone firmly stated. "So . . . I decided to end it."

"To end it." Stone stated and asked at the same time.

"I decided . . . the night before I got here . . . that − in the middle of the night − when everyone was sleeping, I would get up, take whatever booze I could find . . . walk into the woods at the end of our street . . . get as drunk as I could, and swallow the whole blasted bottle of Seroquel that the doctor had prescribed that afternoon − 29 dreadful days worth."

The two men sat quietly for a long moment.

Slowly, Ezra asked, "Did you do it?"

"I . . . I . . .," Stone stuttered and stopped . . . "I . . . don't remember . . . but, I'm sure . . ."

"Sure? . . . Sure of what?"

Stone stared away from Ezra and frowned.

"Sure that you're in hell?" Ezra asked.

"Yeah," Stone said quietly, but firmly, stunned that Ezra was actually listening and acknowledging − validating what anyone else would have called madness.

"So . . . what am I doing here − in hell?" Ezra smiled with all sincerity.

"Sent to torture me − with a futile plan for getting out."

"Okay," Ezra said, "That's plausible."

Stone squinted his eyes, his head shaking. He was again stunned that Ezra wasn't telling him how wrong he was. But he quickly realized that Ezra's going along might all be part of the torture.

"You *believe* me?" Stone said incredulously.

"I said it's plausible," Ezra replied. "From your perspective − in your experience − it is plausible."

"But you don't believe it."

"Doesn't matter what I believe. In your experience, it's perfectly plausible – and very real – deadly real."

"It's real, all right."

"But not certain," Ezra cocked a wry smile.

"Huh?"

"You can't *know*."

"Know what?"

"That you killed yourself - and are now burning in everlasting Hell." Ezra answered.

"Maybe that's part of the torture . . . Not *knowing* . . . Not being *able* to know – either way."

"That's plausible," Ezra said again, "in your experience . . . But you said, 'Maybe' . . . 'Maybe that's part of the torture' . . . Maybe." Ezra smiled.

"Yeah."

"That 'maybe' means you don't know."

"I don't know how I can know – or if I can know – but I know what I'm going through." Stone insisted.

"It feels like Hell – the real thing. Literally." Ezra nodded hard and earnestly.

"Yeah."

"But *maybe* it isn't," Ezra kindly grinned. "Right?"

"Yeah."

"So, you've got nothing to lose by choosing to believe that you *do* have a chance – in a *metaphorical* hell."

Stone stared, not knowing what to say. It was all so nutcase absurd.

"And that my grand-loony plan could work!" Ezra laughed heartily out-loud.

"Yeah . . . *maybe*," Stone laughed back.

"Now there ya go!" Ezra boomed and beamed.

"What?" Stone said, puzzled by Ezra's glee.

"You laughed!" Ezra charged, crazily raising his brow and grinning.

"Yeah," Stone shrugged.

"You think there's any laughing in hell?"

Stone shrugged again, raised his brow, and didn't have an answer.

"And how about that tiny spark of hope you felt when you agreed to the plan? . . . You think that would happen in hell? . . . Is there hope in hell?"

"Don't know," Stone said, "Not any *real* hope . . . I guess."

"Yes! Yes! Yes!" Ezra cheered. "You don't know . . . so *maybe* it's time to choose to decide to believe that *maybe* you are still alive and there is a chance that you might walk through this hell – and live!"

"It's hard," Stone said, wanting to choose to decide to believe in a 'maybe.'

"Hell, yeah, it's hard!" Ezra boomed and grinned and clowned.

"You think there's hope . . . for me?"

"I gave you the plan, didn't I?"

"Yeah . . . but—

"But nothin'," Ezra snapped. "Show me that I'm not wastin' my time. What did you read this morning?"

Stone did not have to pick up the booklet. The words were still in his head.

"When you pray, do not use a lot of meaningless words, as the pagans do, who think that God will hear because their prayers are long. Don't be like them. Your Father already knows what you need before you ask him."[3]

Ezra wasted no time. "What sticks out to you in those words?" he asked.

"God knows how to get me out of this hell."

"Yes He does indeed!" Ezra crowed maniacally.

"What's stoppin' him?" Stone asked, wistfully lifting his voice.

"Excellent question!" Ezra pounced. "It may not be his will for you to be here . . . but there is no doubt that He has allowed you to go through this and He has not taken you out."

"I do deserve to be here. I know that I've screwed everything up. Hurt people. *Sinned*, I guess – every day of my life," Stone struggled to say it, but he said it differently now. He was working confusedly – curiously – trying to figure a way to hope.

"You know I'm not going to deny any of that," Ezra stated firmly; unwilling to coddle.

"But you're telling me – that passage is telling me – that God knows how to get me out of here. To help me. To heal my mind. To get me out of this hell . . . I need to know what's stoppin' him."

"There's more to this than just getting' out," Ezra nodded. "Tell me that first line again."

"When you pray –[4]

"Stop!" Ezra blasted . . . "How much-a that you been doin'"

"I'm not sure I even know how anymore," Stone said, letting out a long deep breath.

"Well, let's start with what Jesus just told you. 'Do not use a lot of meaningless words' . . . Don't go babbling on and on, like some people do."

"Okay. So what do I say?" Stone asked.

"Doesn't matter so much *what* you say as *who* you say it to . . . Remember, He already knows what you need . . . "How about you start with 'My Father in heaven, I praise you . . .'"

"That might be harder than it sounds," Stone said honestly.

"Yeah!" Ezra barked. "So, force yourself! . . . And you'll be prayin'."

"Then what?"

"You listen . . . And maybe you don't hear anything . . . So, you sit there – just . . . sit there . . . and know – or force yourself to choose to *'make-believe'* - that He is with you. And spend time with Him . . . Maybe in complete silence."

"Okay . . . Why not?" Stone easily agreed. "Complete silence would be a nice change."

"Here," Ezra said, "Take this," and handed Stone a wire-bound set of '3by5' index cards.

"What's this for?"

"Write down. Everyday. In just a couple sentences. Your own words . . . what you got out of the day's reading."

Stone paused.

"Go ahead," Ezra commanded, "Do it now . . . I want to be sure you don't forget."

Stone grabbed a pen and opened to the first card.

"Force myself to spend time with God. He already knows how to break me out of Hell."

"Read that passage in the booklet again tonight, before you go to bed," Ezra said and headed out of the room.

"I will," Stone committed.

"And listen!" Ezra barked from just outside of Stone's door. "When that blasted sodomite voice raises up inside your head, you tell it to go back to hell" he ordered. "You say, 'In Jesus' Name, I <u>command</u> you back to hell – where you belong.' Got it?"

And Ezra Eliot Loleko was gone.

And Stone sat alone. "My Father . . . I . . . *praise* you?" he whispered and shrugged; not having the slightest clue what might happen next. And he wondered whether he should choose to decide . . . to, maybe, hope. Even a little.

DAY FOUR

"JESUS SAW THE CROWDS AND WENT UP A HILL, WHERE He sat down. His disciples gathered around him and He began to teach them . . ."[5]

"Two sentences? That's it?" Stone groused, after opening the booklet first thing the next morning – just as planned. "What am I supposed to do with that?"

It was an excellent question. And the answer was more obvious than he realized.

"Jesus saw the crowds and went up a hill, where He sat down."[6]

"Okay. Doesn't seem like much there." Stone smirked and rolled his eyes. "He saw a bunch of people and He climbed a hill. Why do I need to know that? Why did He climb the hill? Why did He sit down? Does any of it make a difference? I could guess," he thought, "but it doesn't say."

"His disciples gathered around him and He began to teach them."[7]

"Yeah," Stone shrugged. "He was a teacher. That's what He did. I knew that. But these two sentences don't say a blasted thing about what He taught, so, . . . Aw, forget it!" he barked. "How am I supposed to get anything out of this? It's ridiculous."

He stood up, threw the booklet down on the metal chair beside his bed, and tramped off to the bathroom, wearing a tight, hard frown.

"What does that lunatic think I'm going to get out of this?" Stone whispered.

He was frustrated. But he didn't realize what that frustration meant. He _wanted_ to get something out of the passage. And that meant his hope had gone beyond the bare flicker that got him to doubtfully agree to give Ezra's program a 'what-have-I-got-to-lose' chance in the first place.

"One meaningless sentence," Stone thought, "and another that didn't tell me anything I don't already know . . . What's the use? I did what I said I would do. I read it. I thought about it. And I'll do it again this afternoon."

He went to breakfast and chewed the scripture out of his mind. But his mind – or something – wouldn't let it go. Back there, somewhere, his brain – or something – kept working on it.

"Jesus saw the crowds and He went up a hill and sat down and taught them."[8]

"Yeah, so? . . . What? _What_ did He teach them?"

Stone knew – or believed or, maybe, imagined– that Ezra wasn't going to waste those two sentences. He'd have something – even if he had to make it up. And it nagged Stone. Some part of his brain or soul or spirit – or something - wanted to get it before he talked with Loleko. And that something kept bringing the seemingly meaningless scripture back to his mind . . . But something else kept saying, _"You know this is useless, Livingstone . . . There ain't no getting out of here . . . There ain't no rest for the wicked."_ And, today, that second voice was in the lead.

———————————— ⑂ ————————————

"He-l-l-l-o-o-o-h! Hallel-u-u-u-jah Livingst-o-o-o-ne!" Ezra sang, and bellowed, and smiled; eyes flashing, looking happier than any man locked on a psych ward should have had any reason to choose to be. "What's happening this fine afternoon, my friend?"

Ezra was obviously in less of a hurry to get down to business than Stone.

"Two sentences," Stone smirked, not quite playfully.

"Ah, yes. Jesus went up a hill and taught his disciples."

"Ah, yes, Stone mimicked," a little more playfully. "What am I supposed to get out of that?" he halfway snapped and halfway grinned.

"An excellent question." Ezra soared, playing along. "Indeed, that _is_ the question."

"It's ridiculous," Stone flashed, without anger. "It doesn't say anything about _what_ He taught. So how am I supposed to get anything out of it?"

"You know," Ezra paused, winked, grinned goofily, and raised his brow, "The full question is 'What are you supposed to get out of _what God is telling you_ in those sentences?'"

"Not much," Stone declared with haste.

"A-a-h-h-h . . . _a-a-a-l-l_ scripture is Spirit-breathed and useful . . ." Ezra crooned.

"You're in a singing mood, today, aren't you Mr. Loleko?"

"Why not? . . . I can't feel bad when I'm singing . . . Even when I'm moanin' the blues."

Stone just shook his head.

"Read those two sentences for me, Mr. Livingstone."

And Stone obliged – almost willingly.

"_Jesus saw the crowds and he went up a hill and sat down. His disciples gathered around him, and He began to teach them._"[9]

"You know that God is saying something in there, right?" Ezra asked and declared at the same time.

"I'm hoping."

"Wonderful!" Ezra exclaimed. "We could stop right there. You're getting more and more of that, aren't you, Mr. Livingstone?"

"More of what?" Stone bristled.

"Hope."

Stone hadn't realized and it didn't quite seem to apply here. "I hadn't noticed," he panned.

"Do you know how dreadfully miserable you were when we met?"

"Still, pretty much, am."

"Pretty much?! That's a phrase people use when they are trying to bamboozle themselves – and/or somebody else."

"You said I was dreadfully miserable, when we first met," Stone protested at the notion that he wasn't being fully truthful, "And I still - pretty much - am."

"Yes! Yes. Pretty much. That's it!...You've dropped the dreadful . . . Now, you're just miserable.

Stone laughed, which, he realized, proved Loleko's point.

"Tell me what God is saying in those two sentences," Ezra pushed.

"I don't know.

"That's okay," Ezra nodded and grinned, "Tell me what you would say if you did know."

Stone bristled, again. "I'd say Jesus climbed a blasted hill, sat down, and taught his disciples something about which I don't have a clue."

"All true," Ezra smiled.

"Well, there you go. I'll write that down on the index card and we can be done for the day. Climb. Sit. Teach. Without knowing what in the blazes you're teaching." Stone was now miffed and Loleko knew it.

"Okay," Ezra said gently, "Enough of my messing around. You're focused on what <u>Jesus</u> said and did and ---"

"Yes!" Stone barked, cutting him short. "I'm focused on Jesus. Isn't that where I'm supposed to be?"

"Yes . . . and that is just what the disciples did in those two sentences."

Stone looked again and saw what he had missed.

"His disciples gathered around him . . ."[10] Stone said softly.

"There ya go," said Ezra.

"Okay. But isn't that pretty much what the first day's reading said – pray, spend time with God?"

"Pretty much?" Ezra grinned, his eyes twinkling madly.

"Yeah . . . 'Pretty much,'" Stone laughed, "But not exactly, huh?"

"What did Jesus do *before* the disciples gathered around him," Ezra asked, still twinkling.

"I already said," Stone shot, "He climbed a blasted hill."

"Yes! Yes!" Ezra enthused as if he had come upon some great revelation.

"Yes! Yes!" Stone mimicked. "Big deal . . . He climbed a hill."

"Yes! . . . And what did the disciples do after Jesus climbed that hill?"

"They gathered around him," Stone exasperatedly sighed.

"No-No,"Ezra quickly corrected. "Read between the lines. Before they gathered around him . . ."

"Before they gathered around him, they might have been playing tiddly-winks, for all I know," Stone laughed. "The reading doesn't say."

"Before they gathered around him – genius," Ezra teased encouragingly, "they had to climb the hill *after* him."

"I suppose they did," Stone said rolling his eyes, "And, again – big deal!"

"I know," Ezra said gently, "This doesn't sound like anything much at all . . . But you're wanting Jesus to do something big. You want Him to get you out of hell . . . And He will . . . But you don't just get out of hell . . . You gotta have somewhere to go when you get out - and you can't go back to where you used to be . . . There's someplace else you gotta go."

"Oh, yeah," Stone objected, "Where's that?"

"Wherever Jesus leads."

"And . . . I suppose," Stone groaned, almost playfully, "He

wants me to go follow along without having any clue where's He's leading . . . right?"

Ezra shrugged. "It's gotta be someplace better than hell . . . right?"

Stone paused . . . "I can't really argue with that," he curiously smiled . . . stared, and shook his head. "But I still want to know what he taught them at the top of that hill," Stone demanded.

"Good!" Ezra firmly, gleefully – and goofily – nodded, reaching into his pocket. "Lucky for you, I've got it right here."

And Stone read the words that Ezra handed him.

"Happy the man who . . ." [11]

Hallelujah dropped his head. He had not been happy in a long time.

"If I want to get out of this hell," Stone wrote on his index card, "I'm going to have to follow Jesus _wherever_ he leads."

"You know this passage you read today, Mr. Livingstone," Ezra paused. "That wasn't the only hill that Jesus climbed."

Stone stared and re-opened his index cards.

"This ain't gonna be easy," he wrote.

DAY FIVE

"WHERE DID YOU COME FROM?" HALLELUJAH ASKED EZRA when they met that afternoon.

"The womb. Just like everybody else," Ezra cackled, getting a kick out of himself.

Stone shook his head, smirked, and laughed – just a little. "No kidding, idiot." he snapped playfully. "Where were you born and raised?"

"Cincinnati. Land of the Gambling-Banned Hit King."

"Pete Rose."

"Yeah. Cincinnati. Part North. Part South. All Midwest . . . Just across the Ohio from Honest Abe's home state. Everything to love and hate about 'fly-over country' – all in one place . . . But what difference does it make?"

"You don't like the city?" Stone asked.

"I don't dislike it. But I don't have any special affinity for the place just because I happened to be born there . . . I never understood that kind of thing . . . I could live anywhere else and be just as happy. Leave anywhere, too."

"You mentioned Pete Rose."

"Yep. Gambled himself right out of the Hall of Fame," Ezra

quipped. "Of course, in all honesty, there ain't nobody worthy of being enshrined in *any* Hall of Fame."

"I kinda understand Rose."

"Yeah? How do you understand him?" Ezra asked.

"Well . . . y'know . . . I gave up the best opportunity I'm probably ever gonna have."

Ezra sensed that Hallelujah wanted him to say something. He had some way of "sensing." But he also sensed that Hallelujah was on the verge of something that had been eating at him for some time – maybe a long time. So, he did the best thing he could . . . He kept his mouth shut.

And, just as Ezra expected, the silent tension got Stone to re-open his.

"Y'know why I asked you about your hometown?" Stone said, not looking for an answer. "I was a pitcher. Baseball. Went to Vanderbilt University on a baseball scholarship. Screwed that up good - and paid to go to another school -and pitch," Stone shook his head. "I got drafted by the Minnesota Twins – late rounds."

"Sounds like you were pretty darn good," Ezra complimented simply and honestly – and without any trace of a fan's awe.

"I was pitching for a team in Hickory . . . North Carolina – Single-A, minor league baseball . . . My first year as a pro – My *only* year as a pro . . ."

Stone paused and Ezra nodded. "Hickory. You were a pro, that one year," Ezra said in a skilled way that was somehow encouraging.

Stone went on.

Ezra could see that this was hard for Stone, but he didn't know why. So he listened. And Stone felt Ezra listening, but he didn't realize that was why he had been able to bring this up in the first place.

"I was really getting the job done," Stone said with more sorrow than pride. "My fastball was up to 94 mph. That's big in Single-A. And my slider was working . . . Just a coupla weeks into the season, the manager, Wally Burgess – he was about 70 and still hangin' in there in the low minors, musta loved the game . . . or maybe he was afraid to quit – anyway, he made me his closer. I was comin' in with the game on the line in the ninth inning and blowin' 'em away."

"You were gettin' the job done," Ezra smiled softly and nodded. "94 mile per hour fastball. Good slider. Sounds like a tough combination for a Single-A hitter to face."

"I was 8-for-8 in save opportunities in my first month. 15 strikeouts in 12 innings, only two walks, and one lousy homerun that the wind pushed out of a bandbox park in Myrtle Beach."

"What was your FIP?"

"My FIP?!" Stone shrieked.

"Yeah," Ezra slyly grinned. "Fielding Independent Pitching."

Stone was shocked. "You know this stuff?" he exclaimed, wide-eyed. "Sabermetrics . . . Advanced baseball stats."

"Some, yeah. They're hated by scouts and fans alike – most of 'em, anyway."

"They're new," Stone said, "and baseball loves tradition – even when it proves to be dead wrong."

"They'll catch on," Ezra nodded. "The stat geeks are changing the game – for the better. So, what was your FIP?"

"Don't remember . . . It was good. But I don't remember."

"Give me a minute," Ezra said, reaching to the table beside Stone's bed for a pen and paper, and scribbled some numbers. "2.70!" he proudly declared. "That's good. But your xFIP was even better."

"I know," Stone barked. "xFIP adjusts for that lousy bandbox of a park that turned a pop-up to right into a homerun."

"Yeah. But that cheap homer isn't what's on your mind," Ezra encouraged.

"Hacked me off good. But it doesn't mean anything now . . . Y'know, I looked great out there . . . 6-foot-6, 225 pound, 22-year-old closer, with a mid-90's two-seamer. Getting' easy outs . . ." Stone trailed away and stared at something far off, up and to his left.

"You looked great out there . . . But there's something about it that's still eatin' at you four years later."

"Blast it, man!" Stone snapped. "Nobody could see it . . . They saw me lookin' great. They figured I had the world by the backside – And I did! . . . There was no way they could see it."

"See what?"

"It's why . . . I asked you about your hometown . . . I looked great . . . . but I was comin' apart. Nobody could tell. I guess I hid it . . . or maybe they just couldn't imagine a 6-foot-6-inch closer . . ." he grit his teeth and turned hard away from Ezra . . . who said nothing.

Stone shook his head, as if to knock something out of it that he didn't want to think about. And didn't want to say; had never said.

"I had the world by the tail, man!" he growled and yelled . . . "Blowin' hitters away. They couldn't touch me – and I was comin' apart inside, the whole blasted time. As soon as I got there."

"What happened, Stone?" Ezra quietly – gently – pushed.

"I was hearin' it already . . . in my head. *'You're no crankin' good . . . You screwed up everything you ever touched and you're gonna screw up this . . . Look at how you treat people! You don't care about anything – or anybody – except yourself. Yeah, sure, you're nice to some people – to get something out of them – or make yourself look good. You wicked . . .'* And I couldn't stop it."

"Sounds like hell," Ezra said. "It *was* hell," he nodded firmly. "Sounds like – sometimes – it's *still* hell . . . but you said it had something to do with why you asked me about my hometown . . . What's that about?"

"I quit!" Stone barked angrily. "I quit on the best chance I'll ever have . . . right when I was really makin' it . . . And went home . . . It was _all_ I wanted – to go back home. To get back to mom and dad, where . . .?

"Where what?"

"Where it was safe! Safe?! . . . My heavens," Stone sighed.

"6-foot-6-inch, 225-pound grown-man, sissy closer ran back to mommy - in the middle of the season!"

Ezra sat there and let it all sink in – for him *and* Stone.

Stone hung his head and banged his fist unknowingly against his knee.

Ezra finally interrupted.

"You ran home, Stone, because hell was chasing you."

"Why? . . . Why was hell chasing me?"

"There's a battle raging all around you, Stone . . . You can't see it, but it's been going on for years."

"What're you talkin' about?" Stone winced and objected.

"What scripture passage did you read today – in the booklet?" Ezra asked.

"It was short," Stone said, "but I don't remember it exactly. Let me get it," he said. And he began to read.

"The wicked will have to suffer,"[12] Stone twitched,

"but those who trust in the Lord

Are protected by his constant love."[13]

"That's the war that's been raging all around you – for years. . . Those voices in your head," Ezra said, startling Stone, "They're not voices – not like what you think they are."

"How do you know about that – the voices?"

"It's a gift," Ezra said without arrogance. "Those are not psychotic *voices*. Those are voices of spiritual warfare . . . They're fighting it out on the battleground of your soul."

"What? Like an angel on one shoulder and a devil on the other, whispering in my ears?"

"No," Ezra exclaimed. "This isn't a cartoon. This is very real – and deadly serious. More real and serious than anything you've ever known . . . It's demons sent from hell, trying to drag you into the pit . . . And the Holy Spirit of God, trying to win your soul to eternal life."

"You really believe this stuff? Demons and spirits and angels - fighting over my *soul*? . . . Sounds nuts."

"Look at the shape you're in. That ain't no accident. This <u>war</u> . . . is at the breaking point." Ezra declared.

"The demons must be winning."

"You have to play your part!"

"What's that?" Stone asked. My part? What am *I* supposed to do -- with demons and angels and spirits?"

"What's the scripture say?"

"*Those who trust in the Lord are protected by his constant love,*"[14] Stone frowned – and smiled – and frowned again.

DAY SIX

STONE'S HEAD JERKED HARD TO THE LEFT AND BACK toward his right shoulder. His face and neck twitched. He groaned and writhed and threw himself backward. He let the booklet fall to the floor.

The first couple of passages he had read gave Stone the only minutes of peace that he could find – even if that peace left a moment after he put the booklet down. So, he was looking forward to reading today. Looking forward to that peace. But these verses – today – just enflamed the horror. He was hurled back into every wicked thing his brain – or something – had been telling him since long before he ever laid eyes on Ezra Eliot Loleko.

"From deep in the world of the dead... down into the depths... banished from your presence... into the land whose gates lock shut forever."[15]

"This was no coincidence," Stone's mind blazed.

Those lines were shot right at him. Made to cut. Made to taunt. Made to laugh at him. And the cutting, taunting, and laughing had been raging in his mind for hours now.

"What in the weary-wide world happened to you?" Ezra busted out as soon as he saw Stone.

"Whad'a'ya mean?"

"You're twitchin' and shakin' all over. You're a wreck." Ezra was not one to mince words. "It's 2:00 in the afternoon and you're wearin' the clothes you slept in. You haven't combed your hair. Haven't cleaned up at at all. And probably didn't brush your teeth."

That was all pretty typical symptomatology for a severely depressed man – and there was no mistaking Stone, today, for anything other than a severely depressed – and terrified – man. He had been able to fake it, but not so well recently – and not all today.

"What's going on?" Ezra asked more politely, but still without any hint of the balderdash that people use to politely side-step the pain of the human being in front of them.

"*You threw me down into the depths,*" Stone said slowly, "*into the land whose gates lock shut forever – Deep in the world of the dead*"[16] He didn't need to look at the booklet. Didn't need to read those words. This was one little part of scripture that he had thoroughly seared into his memory.

"*That*! Yes, yes!" Ezra boomed. "The land whose gates lock shut forever. Yes . . . that is where you think you are."

"Yeah. You knew that . . . And you knew that I was going to be reading those lines today. And *you* are asking *me* what's going on?"

Ezra heard Stone. He always heard everything Stone had to say to him. But he continued as if Stone had not said a word. "And you believe God threw you there . . . into the depths, the world of the dead."

"I *am* dead . . . or . . . if not . . . as good as dead."

"And you're getting what you deserve . . . right?"

"Yeah."

"Why else would God throw you deep into the world of the dead . . . right!" Ezra wasn't asking. He was telling Stone what he was thinking. He knew.

Stone bit his upper light and jerked his head quickly, left then right."

"That's what you're thinking. Again. Still. Isn't it?" Ezra wasn't going to let up. It was time to push. "Why did God throw you down deep into the land of the dead?"

"Because I screwed up!" Stone barked, then quickly caught himself. "Because I made a mess of my life. Because I'm evil and I got this comin' to me."

"That's all true," Ezra said calmly, without hesitation, and firmly.

Stone stared. He didn't say anything. He was again surprised that Ezra wasn't trying to change his seemingly psychotic mind . . . And that made him listen.

You _do_ have it comin'. This _is_ what you deserve. But you're missing something."

He was keeping Stone curious. He was up to something. Stone knew that. Ezra was always up to something. Nothing was wasted. But Stone couldn't figure this.

"What am I missing?" Stone snapped, with a quick-jabbing lift of his brow and thrust of his chin; as if to say, "I ain't missin' a blazin' thing!"

"We _all_ deserve it, " Ezra exulted, almost laughing. "We've all got it comin'."

"Listen, man," Stone said intensely, quietly – almost angrily – and gravely. "I believe in God now more than I ever have. I know that He is real. But this ain't no joke. I've got this coming. I've been evil. Am evil. And the only reason God would put me in the land of the dead . . . was if he had already locked the gates shut forever. . . This is why I _know_ that He's real now . . . He's angry as hell with me and he wouldn't throw me down, banish me, and lock the gates - forever - behind me . . . unless I had it comin' and there was no way out . . . He's done with me!"

"That's where you're wrong."

Stone lowered his head and stared silently at the floor. He wasn't having any of what he thought Ezra might be selling. Some madman's nonsense about it never being too late.

"Read the whole passage," Ezra instructed.

Stone quivered. And his voice quaked as he read.

"From deep in the world of the dead I cried for help, and you heard me. You threw me down into the depths, to the very bottom of the sea, where the waters were all around me, and all your mighty waves rolled over me".[17] Stone twitched and jerked.

"I thought I had been banished from your presence and would never see your holy Temple again."[18] Stone gasped and faintly felt a swelling tear, but he couldn't cry.

"The water came over me and choked me; the sea covered me completely, and seaweed wrapped around my head. I went down to the very roots of the mountains, into the land whose gates lock shut forever."[19]

Stone groaned achingly out loud. "I'm a dead man."

"You're not finished," Ezra said, "Go on."

"But you, O Lord my God, brought me back from the depths alive. When I felt my life slipping away, then O Lord, I prayed to you, and in your holy Temple you heard me."[20]

Stone sighed hard and Ezra looked directly at him.

"What makes you think you're sin is greater than Jonah's?"

"Huh?" Stone winced.

"That's where those words come from . . . The book of Jonah . . . Jonah prayed those words. What makes you think your sin is greater than his was?"

"What was Jonah's sin?" Stone asked.

"God gave him a direct command to preach to the people of Nineveh . . . And, instead, he ran away."

"So, Jonah disobeyed God one time," Stone said ruefully, "I've been evil my whole life."

"I could show you," Ezra firmly grinned, "that no one sin is greater than any other and that they all deserve the death penalty. But I don't think you're gonna hear that right now. You'd still be convinced that there is no way for you to escape and have life again – real life – for the first time."

"Probably not."

"But I can show you that Jonah – with that one sin – had it comin', just like you."

Stone blinked toward the floor and looked back at Ezra.

"Jonah disobeyed God's command to preach to Nineveh . . . Now that might not sound so serious . . . Maybe a lot of preachers don't preach what God wants them to preach . . . But what did God want Jonah to preach to Nineveh?"

"I don't have a clue," Stone muttered. "I mean, it's not that I don't know anything about God, but I'm pretty new to this bible reading stuff."

"God commanded Jonah to preach a message of repentance to Nineveh . . . A message of repentance that was the *only* way for the people of that city to save their souls."

"And Jonah didn't do it."

"Not only did Jonah not do it; he didn't do it specifically because Nineveh was an enemy to his people and Jonah did not want God to save the lives and souls of the people of Nineveh . . . He wanted them to burn in Hell – or whatever he thought their punishment might be."

"That's pretty bad," Stone nodded.

"Pretty bad?!" Ezra yelped. "You're sufferin' some kind of hell here. But you're only one person . . . Jonah wanted the whole blasted city to burn – eternally! And he defied God, hoping to make it happen," Ezra, strangely, cackled out loud.

"What's so funny?" Stone couldn't help but grin.

"What, now, makes you think that your sin is greater than Jonah's sin?"

"Maybe it's not . . . But what difference does it make? Maybe me and Jonah are in the same burning boat of damnation."

"Not quite," Ezra smiled. "You and Jonah both got thrown out of the same blasted boat, but you're still at *the very bottom of the sea . . . down into the depths . . . into the land whose gates lock shut forever.*"[21]

"Yeah, and—

"And Jonah isn't!" Ezra boomed. "He was – but he isn't any more. He got out of his hell! And if Jonah can – who was just as bad, if not worse than you – then _you_ can get out, too!"

Stone shook his head and jerked. _"Bull! Nonsense!"_ Someone said in his brain. _"You're wicked . . ."_

"In Jesus' Holy Name," Ezra roared, when he saw Stone twitch, "I command you back to Hell where you belong! . . . In Jesus' Name, get out of here, you lying, curs-ed fraud."

Stone leaped like he had been hit with an electric cattle prod. "What?! Me?" he buzzed.

"No!" Ezra roared again. "That forever condemned demon, bearing false witness in your head."

"I . . . I," Stone stuttered uncertainly, wanting to believe. "I wish he would go away forever."

"Don't wish!" Ezra blasted. "Pray! . . . _Pray – and_ command!" he raged. _"Command_ that demon, in Jesus' Holy Name, to be gone from you every time he opens his lying mouth!"

"Wow," was all Stone could say.

"Now, Hallelujah Livingstone!" Ezra boomed, still cranking from his blitzkrieg on Gahenna's goon, "How did Jonah get out of _"the land whose gates lock shut forever."_[22] How did he come _back from the depths alive when he felt his life slipping away?"_[23]

"He prayed?" Stone answered uneasily, as if guessing, but thinking he was probably right.

"Yeah, he prayed," Ezra said, still booming, but unsatisfied . . . "But he didn't _just_ pray," Ezra roared. "This wasn't some sissy whisper. This man was desperate . . . This man was in the land whose gates lock shut forever – at least, that's where he was in his mind – just like you . . . In his mind, he was in hell. This wasn't some silent, 'Oh, God, please, if it's okay with you, um, could you . . . please help me please.' No!" Ezra roared. "He cried out! . . . He yelled – out loud – like he was about to be set ablaze and needed to get out – Now! . . . Jonah let out a roar! This was the raging – out loud – desperate, last chance, _groaning_, booming, _growl_ of a dying man who had no other hope!"

Stone just stood and stared.

"_That_ is how you need to pray . . . That is how you need to cry out to God . . . Groaning with everything you've got in that 6-foot-6 inches and 225 pounds that He's given you.

That night, Stone groaned and roared and cried out beyond himself – caring only that God heard; unconcerned with what the nurses and aides might think. It was a nuthouse, he figured. They gotta take this kind of thing for granted.

DAY SEVEN

"HAPPY ARE THOSE WHOSE SINS ARE FORGIVEN, WHOSE wrongs are pardoned. Happy is the man whom the Lord does not accuse of doing wrong and who is free from all deceit.

When I did not confess my sins, I was worn out from crying all day long. Day and night you punished me, Lord; my strength was completely drained, as moisture is dried up by the summer heat.

Then I confessed my sins to you; I did not conceal my wrongdoings. I decided to confess them to you, and you forgave all my sins . . .[24]

. . . The Lord says, "I will teach you the way you should go; I will instruct you and advise you. Don't be stupid like a horse or a mule, which must be controlled with a bit and bridle to make it submit.[25]

The wicked will have to suffer, but those who trust in the Lord are protected by his constant love. You that are righteous, be glad and rejoice because of what the Lord has done. You that obey him, shout for joy!"[26]

So much of that passage was about salvation, sin, confession, love . . . forgiveness. All of which Hallelujah Livingstone desperately needed. But, in his present state of mind, Stone saw just one word.

"Submit."

There was nothing in Hallelujah Livingstone that wanted to submit to anything – ever. He had been fighting since he was a kid; even when he had no clue that he was fighting, or what he was fighting for – or against – and, sometimes, even why.

Stone was kind and considerate. A real gentlemen. Most of the time. But he banged against authority ever since that day when he was 15 years old and a zealous, young coach yanked and shook his facemask for the crime of having ferociously blocked – and rolled over – the wrong linebacker.

Stone hung his head and walked back to the practice-field huddle, shamed. Later, he vowed that it would never happen again. Nobody would ever again get away with treating him like that. And the next time the coach tried it – three weeks later – the already 6-foot-four-inch, 210-pound Hallelujah Livingstone was thrown off of the team. Football coaches don't take kindly to being slugged by a sophomore.

Submitting was not a part of Hallelujah Livingstone, but, in the middle of this hell, the fight was 95% gone out of him. He had beaten himself to death and he just felt wrong – about everything.

"You don't need to ask today," Stone said immediately, when he saw Ezra that afternoon.

Loleko's eyes shined and squinted with a peculiar, small, tight grin.

"You know what that passage was. And you know what hit me," Stone barked, somehow gently.

"It ain't easy," Ezra nodded and cocked his head playfully.

"I'm tired."

"You should be," Ezra quickly replied.

Stone did not understand. "It doesn't seem right," he said. "I don't know how to do this."

"I know."

"Know what?"

"Submitting."

Stone stared, hoping – knowing – that Ezra had more to say.

"There ain't anything about you that says submitting is the thing to do. It feels backward. Just the opposite of what you think you need to do."

"What do I think I need to do," Stone said, a little miffed that Ezra – again – presumed to know what was going on in his head.

"What you've been doing all along – almost right up until you couldn't take it anymore and decided to come in here."

"Fighting," Stone said in an angry and broken way, "And losing."

Ezra moved on. "Why did you come in here? Why did you admit yourself?"

"I don't know . Maybe I quit. Maybe I was afraid I was going to quit big time . . . Forever . . . Permanent."

Ezra smiled softly. "You gave in a lot – to keep yourself from giving up completely."

"I didn't want to take myself out!" Stone growled, fast and fierce. "I couldn't do it. I couldn't commit suicide . . . and I couldn't go on living."

"And, yet, here you are."

"I can't keep fighting and . . . submitting feels all wrong . . . and . . ."

"And what?" Ezra demanded.

Stone bit his teeth down hard and frowned angry. "Smack it!" he barked. "I don't want to be stupid like a horse or a mule!"

"No. That's not it," Ezra objected. "You don't want to be controlled with a bit and bridle."

"Blazin', no, I don't!" Stone growled hard. "What is this?!"

"God."

"God?!" Stone snapped.

"That's right. This is all God."

"It feels like hell . . . It feels like a bit and bridle and worse."

47

"Yes! Yes!" Ezra beamed exultation. "Yes, praise God, it is a bit and bridle. And you needed worse."

"What?" Stone shook and squinted with disbelief. But it made sense.

"It's not what you think it is," Ezra went on. "You're not being punished."

Stone was coming not to be amazed at Ezra's ability to discern what he was thinking. He almost expected it. But he still didn't like it.

"This is God's love for you."

"What is?"

"All of this. Everything that you have been going through," Ezra nodded happily, with a turn of his head.

"A hell-fire bit and bridle – and worse – is God's love for me?" Stone quipped and bit, wanting to call Loleko "nuts," but they had been through that before.

"He could have let you destroy yourself. He could have let you cast yourself into Hell – the real thing – with a capitol 'H.' Still could."

"I don't want to be stupid."

"Too late," Ezra smiled; and Stone laughed like a man knowingly standing on his own grave.

"You've had God's bit in your mouth and his bridle strapped around your back for a long time now, Bronco. And you've been fighting and bucking every step of the way."

"I'm sick of it," Stone said in a way that spoke more eloquently than his words.

"He ain't letting go . . . and you can't throw him. Even with all your beating yourself up and calling yourself evil and thinking that you have, somehow, become the very first living, breathing human being to achieve the unachievable feat of sinning bigger and badder than the grace of God."

"What do I do now?" Stone asked, not quite believing that he could do anything, but unable to quench – or turn away from - the hope that leaped from Ezra.

"Cave in," Ezra boomed and beamed. "Be broken. Give up."

Stone laughed woefully. Briefly. And smiled, "Sounds like submitting."

Ezra laughed, still booming and beaming, "Or ride yourself kicking and screaming all the way into Hell."

"The real thing," Stone asked knowingly, "with a capitol 'H'?"

"That's it." Ezra stared and firmly nodded, suddenly looking like he meant business – but not quite serious. He was always sincere – even when he was loonying-off, even when he was telling a tall tale. But he never came off as grave or serious. Ezra Eliot Loleko was filled with too much joy for that.

"How?" Stone asked, almost pleading, wanting to hope, but still not believing that it could all be true for him. "How do I submit?"

"It ain't easy. But it isn't as hard as you think. And you've already been through the worst of it."

"And the rest of it?"

Ezra smiled. "You give your life to Jesus Christ."

"Yeah. I've heard people say that," Stone nodded earnestly. "But it seems a lot bigger – tougher - than they let on."

"And it is!" Ezra loudly lilted, shining like a gleeful madman. "You're surrendering. Giving in. Letting Christ take control. Submitting. Completely. Bigger than you have ever submitted to anything before – except sin."

"You probably think I should leap right into that. Like it's the only logical thing to do," Stone rightly surmised. "You say I've been through the worst it – and maybe I have – but giving my life away . . ." Stone's voice trailed off and he stared at Ezra, but Ezra didn't say anything.

The silence sat between them for a heavy moment, but Ezra wouldn't budge.

"Giving my life away. Giving complete control over my

life . . . over me! To somebody else – even Jesus. Even God himself . . ." he trailed off again. And, again, Ezra said nothing.

"You say I've been through the worst of it," Stone, somehow, stated and asked at the same time.

"You've gone through hell to get to where you are now," Ezra grinned, nodded, and winked; all crookedly.

This time, it was Stone's turn not to say anything – but not like Ezra. When Ezra remained silent, it wasn't because he didn't know what to say.

"You've gone through hell to get to where you are now," Ezra repeated. "It was the only way you were going to get here . . . There are other ways. But you're a fighter. You had to be beaten down to this. And, maybe, built up to it at the same time."

"There have to be better ways."

"There are easier ways," Ezra said, with a crazy, bright-eyed frown. "But you might have chosen the best way."

"Huh?"

"Ever hear of St. Paul," Ezra quizzed.

"I remember hearing his name at Mass, 'A reading from the letter of St. Paul to the Pelaponetian Heathens,'" Stone incongruently joked.

"Thanks be to God," Ezra correctly replied. "Paul persecuted Christians, not long after Jesus ascended into heaven – and he believed that he was serving God by doing it."

Stone shook his head. "So, you're telling me that the best way to get to the point of putting your faith in Christ is to persecute Christians . . . ? I know you're nuts – or you wouldn't be in here, but that's insane."

Ezra laughed. "That's not what I'm saying."

"Sure sounds like it."

"I'm saying that, sometimes, God wants a man with the passion and intensity of Paul. One who madly believes what he believes and doesn't give in."

"I thought I was supposed to give in," Stone quipped.

"Sometimes, God wants a fighter. Sometimes, God wants to do something big – and only a fighter will get it done."

"Why did Paul give in . . . to God, if he was such a fighter."

"Well, sorta the same reason that you are so close to giving in?"

"Paul lost his mind," Stone said, "and thought he had died and gone to hell with no way out?"

"It might not have been that bad," Ezra quickly replied. "Paul had to be hit with lightning, struck down in the middle of the street and blinded before he could hear God and put his faith in Christ. But God had been using his whole life, right up until that moment."

"For what?"

"To prepare him," Ezra replied.

"For what?"

"To witness to just about the whole known world and write maybe three-fifths of the New Testament."

"This is big," Stone whispered to himself, his voice cracking and a tear welling in his eye.

Ezra let that sink in.

"What about all the rules and laws that you gotta follow?" Stone challenged.

"The commandments?"

"Yeah, but all of it. Everything ya have to do to be a Christian."

"Love the Lord your God with all your mind, heart, soul, and strength. And love your neighbor as yourself."

"I ain't been to church in awhile," Stone said, "but I heard a lot more about rules, and laws, and commandments than that."

"Love the Lord your God with all your mind, with all your heart, with all your soul, and with all your strength. And love your neighbor as yourself," Ezra repeated simply.

"That's it."

"Jesus said that summed up the whole law."

"I don't know if I can do that," Stone honestly confessed.

"You can't!" Ezra beamed. "He'll help you. He'll do it in you."

"What about stealing and lying . . . adultery, lusting, and all the rest?"

"You think those things have been good for the world?" Ezra cackled and grinned.

Stone couldn't argue that point.

"Listen," Ezra firmly stated, "If you are loving God with all you got and you're loving your neighbor as yourself, you are going to be doing all the rest of it . . . And God will let you know when you screw up."

"So, I put my faith in Christ . . ." Stone paused. "And God forgives everything."

"Everything!" Stone declared. "Everything – past, present _and future_."

"Sounds like a license to sin."

"You put your whole-hearted faith in <u>Christ</u>," Ezra adamantly proclaimed, "And you won't want to sin."

Stone said nothing. Ezra said nothing. And, for a long time, Stone's eyes glazed as he stared at something far off – his past, his future . . . his hell . . . and his one chance to survive.

For a moment, Ezra disappeared from Stone's awareness, though he was sitting right in front of him – and he refused to interrupt. He just sat there . . . praying silently.

Finally, Stone looked back at Ezra, as if he had just re-entered the room.

"What's it gonna be?!" Ezra demanded.

"What choice do I have? You said God has that bit in my mouth and the bridle around my shoulders. And he isn't letting go. He's already taking control."

"You could keep on riding and bucking through this hell – right on into the real thing."

"Yeah. Be stupid like a horse or a mule . . . or . . . surrender." Stone still gritted at the sound of the word.

"Enough of this beating around the balderdash." Ezra growled and beamed at the same time.

Stone jerked backward, startled.

"Are you a sinner?" Ezra demanded.

Stone didn't know what to say. It was a strange question.

"Are you a sinner," Ezra repeated, as if he had reached the punch-line of a well-told joke.

"Yes," Stone shook his head, as though he were hurriedly saying 'No.' "Of course, I . . . AM . . . a sinner."

"Is Jesus Christ the Son of God?"

Stone stuttered and hesitated and swayed, as if the floor beneath him had shifted . . . Submitting felt like losing his life. But he knew that he needed a miracle. He knew that he needed Jesus Christ to be the Son of God.

"Yes . . . He is." Stone gently, but firmly nodded.

"Did He die on the Cross to pay the death penalty that you deserve for your sins?"

Stone lowered his eyes and slowly nodded, knowing what he deserved.

Ezra wasn't satisfied. "Did Jesus Christ die on the Cross to pay the death penalty that you deserve for your sins," he repeated firmly.

"Yes."

"Did he rise from the dead and ascend back into heaven?"

Hallelujah Livingston wanted it to be true. He desperately wanted to believe that it could all be true – even for him. But, even now, he was still fighting. It all seemed so crazy. And he laughed at that thought when he realized that he was locked up in a nuthouse. "So what if it all sounds crazy?" he unwittingly said out loud.

"Yeah," Ezra boomed with laughter, "So what if it sounds crazy."

"It's true!" Hallelujah barked, hardly believing that he heard the words come out of his mouth. And he backed off, just a little "Yes . . . Jesus rose from the dead. And . . ." he hesitated. "Yes . . . ascended back into heaven."

"Is Jesus Christ the Savior of the World?"

Stone knew that he needed a miracle, but . . . He believed that Jesus could save others, but . . .

"Yes," Stone whispered, "Jesus is the Savior of the World."

"We're not done," Ezra said firmly.

"I know," Stone replied, his hands and voice shaking.

"Is Jesus – <u>Your</u> – Savior? Will you *let* Him be <u>your</u> Lord and Savior? Do you, Hallelujah Livingstone, <u>submit</u> . . . your life . . . to Christ?"

Stone hesitated, again, and rocked as if the whole earth was quaking around him. He was not himself. For a second, it was like he was watching the whole scene from a loft above his room . . . He still half-believed – maybe more – that he was a dead-man, already started on some kind of eternal burn in hell . . . But he felt a small, but undeniable hope ever since he met Ezra Eliot Loleko. And he felt that hope – and more – growing, every time he picked up that little booklet and read a passage from the Word of God. He knew, deep down, that he looked forward to reading it. That it was the only time he felt any peace, at all – other than when he was with Ezra. He needed a miracle and Jesus was the only one he knew in that business.

"Yes. Yes." Stone said firmly, simply – earnestly.

Ezra smiled slightly and kept watching. He didn't say a word.

"I . . . WANT . . . Jesus . . . to be <u>my</u> Lord and Savior! . . . I give my <u>life</u> to Jesus," Stone boldly declared, out loud. "I submit."

"Get on your knees!" Loleko boomed. "I'm going to pray for you, Hallelujah Livingstone!"

And right there, in the middle of a nuthouse bedroom, two nuts dropped to their knees. And Ezra Eliot Loleko prayed like Hallelujah Livingstone had never heard anyone pray before.

That night, Stone wrote only one word in his notebook.

"Submit."

DAY EIGHT

BANG! BANG! IT FELT LIKE 3:00AM IN STONE'S STUPORED brain, as he woke and heaved his body over from one side of the bed to the other.

Bang! The aides and psych nurses were arriving. It was seven in the morning and Stone knew that banging – just like every morning – would keep on and – just like every day – Stone imagined there would be no escaping his brain for the next fourteen hours. But, today, Stone did not wake up depressed or terrified or half-psychotic. On this morning, Stone came off the mattress angry. And not just angry – fighting, raging mad. He had the capacity for the kind of rage that could scare off a wild animal. And this morning *he* was wild with it.

There didn't have to be a reason. Nothing in Stone's physical or natural circumstances had changed. He was still locked in a psych ward. Nobody had paid his financial debts. Nothing had gotten any worse. And the Bang! Bang! Bang! interrupting his sleep every 30 seconds was nothing new. It happened every morning. But today it banged something in Stone's brain that hadn't been there in at least a month – and nobody in that hospital had seen or imagined it.

For no good reason, the dopamine, serotonin, epinephrine and every other chemical in his brain had decided it was time for a fire-fight. His thyroid, pituitary, and the rest of his endocrine system were scrambling hormones to electrify his reactions; and, at the same time, trying to keep the whole power-plant from melting down.

Nothing big had to set Stone off for him to go fighting mad. There didn't have to be a crisis in his life. Nobody had to spit in his face or attack his 60-year-old, loving mother – or even cut him off in traffic. When the chemicals whacked out, Stone raged. All 225 bricked and mortared, well-defined pounds of him.

Most of the time – even in the rage – Stone did a good job of being in control of being out of control. He was, somehow, able to rein it in, just short of causing real damage. Most of the time.

There were rages in which the chemicals did all the work and there were rages in which some fool *did* do something to justify Stone's fury – and the chemicals would take Stone's legitimate response a thousand times beyond where 99% of the world would go.

Of course, there were other times when somebody *could* spit in Stone's face – figuratively or literally – and he wouldn't bat an eye. He'd stare. And he would see something hurting in that other person and that person would see something powerful – and gentle – in Stone; and the whole thing would stop right there.

Today, was not one of those times.

Bang! One more time. And Stone burst through his own door, planted his large frame in the middle of the hall, bared his teeth, and roared! Just roared. No words. Roaring. From deep in his belly, filling his bursting lungs, and exploding with the all-out, growling power of a grizzly kicked in the testicles.

He roared for what seemed like 60 seconds, but was "only" maybe ten. In two blasts of quaking thunder. And then, finally, a boom-growling, "STOP! .... STOP! ... STOP THAT BLASTED BANGING!"

And _everything_ stopped.

For just a moment. Maybe three seconds.

And Stone sprinted to the metal double-doors faster than a 225-pound man ought to be able to sprint. He kicked twice, just beside the knob, and the locked doors exploded open as Stone barreled toward the elevators, with male aides and security personnel scrambling from every direction.

───────────────── ⑅ ─────────────────

Nine hours later, Stone awoke for the second time that day. He tried to sit and was instantly hit with the unmistakable sense that he had fouled up – or, at least, that somebody thought he had fouled up. The leather straps across his chest wasted no time before reminding him of the early morning brawl that landed him where he now lay.

The room was dark – and so was Stone's mind, but not from the thorazine that had thrown the knock-out punch to his nervous system. The darkness in his mind wasn't a medication hangover. It wasn't a brain-stupor headache. It was a "feeling"; an emotion he had not expected.

Stone had no idea how long he had been stoned; no idea what time it was or whether it was even still the same day. But he knew that he had been in seclusion long enough. So, he belted out a wordless roar just to get the attention of a doctor, nurse, or aide.

Sixty seconds passed and Stone roared again. He was not in a most patient mood.

The door opened and an aide peered in. "Good morning, Mr. Livingstone."

"It's still morning?" Stone said, surprised.

"Figure of speech . . . It's 4 o'clock in the afternoon. You've been out for almost nine hours."

"Did anybody get hurt?"

"You bit a guy's arm and threw somebody against the wall when they tried to restrain you and there's a little rug-burn and bump on your forehead. But everybody's good."

"When can I get out of here?" Stone asked.

"About ten minutes after you convince the head nurse that you're not going to explode again."

"No need." Stone declared. "I made my point."

"Yeah. I heard. Stop bangin' the blasted doors at 6 in the morning."

"Can you do me a favor? . . . Since I don't know how long I'm going to be strapped in, can you go to my room and get a booklet that I've been reading? I didn't get to it this morning . . . It's kinda part of my *therapy*."

"I'll ask if you can have it, but I don't see why not."

The aide returned with the booklet and the head nurse a few minutes later.

"I figured it was going to be hard to read with your arms buckled down," the aide smiled, "so I asked Sandy to come back to see if you're ready."

Stone calmly answered a couple of the nurse's questions and that, together with the fact that he wanted to read, gave her the sense that he wasn't likely to do any more damage. But she wasn't completely convinced. She and the aide freed his arms, but the leather straps remained buckled across his chest and legs.

Stone understood that they were being cautious, but he knew that even flat on his back he could do some damage with his fists, if he wanted to.

He didn't. He had made his point. And he wanted to read Ezra's booklet – even in the seclusion room with its literally rubber walls. He felt certain that it would tell him something that he, specifically, needed to hear in that moment.

"I call to the Lord for help; I plead with him. I bring him all my complaints; I tell him my troubles. When I am ready to give up, He knows what I should do."[27]

"Well, Lord," Stone laughed out loud, "I'm strapped to a bed in a loony-bin. I guess I got troubles . . . Help!"

Head Nurse Sandy was obviously – and understandably - in no mood to risk having a mad giant rage up and down her hallways.

Stone didn't get back to his room until 8:00pm. He stretched out a little, threw some cold water on his face, and went looking for Ezra. He had made a commitment and there was still time left in the day to keep it.

"Well, well! Mr. Hallelujah Livingstone," Ezra smiled. "People around here didn't think you had that in you . . . but I know better."

"I woke up with my head throbbing thunder and lighting and I couldn't take them bangin' those blazin', forsaken doors one more second."

"So I heard," Ezra grinned. "You know, the patients are pretty pleased with you for lodging that _complaint_ ."

"Yeah. I lodged a _complaint_," Stone smirked wryly. "I exploded!" he laughed.

"Somebody needed to make that complaint," Ezra said. "They were inconsiderate – probably didn't even realize what they were doing – banging those doors when everybody was sleeping . . . And a lot of people weren't getting any rest at all before they got here."

"I know I wasn't."

"But there are better ways of making a _complaint_," Ezra grinned.

"You're making a point of using that word – _complaint_," Stone surmised.

"Indeed I am, Mr. Livingstone. Indeed I am."

"_I call to the Lord for help,_"[28] Stone said, "_I plead with him. I bring him all my complaints . . . I tell him all my troubles._"[29]

"So, you exploded?!" Ezra laughed.

"Indeed I did, Mr. Loleko. Indeed I did," Stone grinned and nodded.

"Indeed!" Ezra laughed. "And do you know why you woke up in such a miserable disposition?"

"I told you. I was fed up with the banging."

"No," Ezra snapped. "You've been hearing those doors banging at 6:00am since your first morning in this joint."

"True. I guess it was just a bad-brain morning."

"I don't think so."

"You don't say?" Stone smirked playfully and rolled his eyes.

"You woke up feeling miserable," Ezra declared, "because you hacked off your enemy. Angered him up real good."

Stone squinted hard and his face twisted. "That's the strangest thing you've ever said to me."

"Do you know what happened to Jesus right after he was baptized?" Ezra asked.

"No . . . I'm pretty new to this scripture reading program and following Jesus."

"Exactly!"

"I'm sure," Stone shook his head, rolled his eyes, and – again – playfully smirked.

"Right after Jesus was baptized," Ezra said, "the Holy Spirit sent him out into the desert for 40 days – where He was tempted by the Devil."

"The Devil?" Stone said suspiciously.

"Yeah, I know," Ezra grinned. "People might think you're a well-meaning pain in the butt when you talk about God. But deep down – even if they're not believers – something in them wants to know God . . . But . . . when you mention the Devil, well . . . then they figure you're just plain out of your mind."

"I'm past that," Stone winked. "I knew you were out of your mind the moment I met you . . . But that doesn't make you wrong. So, tell me what you're talkin' about."

"Jesus was sent out into the desert and was tempted by the Devil – *right after He was baptized.*"

"So?"

"The Devil saw him get baptized," Ezra said and paused . . . "and he wanted to take Jesus down before He could do any more good . . . And you gave your life to Christ yesterday"

"Yeah . . ." Stone said, confused but curious. "And I woke up miserable today."

"You hacked off the Devil by submitting to Jesus. By asking him to be your Lord and Savior –

"Why would the Devil waste time trying to take me down?" Stone protested.

"You're a dangerous man!"

Stone laughed.

Ezra didn't.

"You gave your life to Christ," Ezra firmly declared, staring straight into Hallelujah's eyes. "The Holy Spirit of God lives inside of you now – He <u>won</u> the battle for your soul . . . That makes you a threat to Satan. And he knows it."

"How did that make me wake up miserable?" Stone wondered honestly.

"He attacked you. He wants to take you down before you can do any good."

"Why didn't God stop him," Stone reasonably asked.

"Good question . . . He could have," Ezra affirmed. "Just like He could have stopped the Devil from tempting Jesus in the desert . . . I don't know why He didn't . . . He has his reasons, of which I sometimes know not . . . But I do know they are all good. And that He is using it to bless you."

"Bless me?!" Stone shrieked. "I exploded and ended up strapped down with thorazine stabbed into my arm . . . Don't sound like no blessing to me."

"You made that choice. And you're no stranger to exploding . . . Maybe God is using this whole attack by the Devil to teach you how to deal with your _complaints_."

Stone didn't say anything. Ezra paused and looked straight at him. A moment passed.

"I call to the Lord for help,"[30] Stone said, repeating the verse he had read while strapped down in the seclusion room. _"I plead with him. I bring him all my complaints. . . I tell him all my troubles."_[31]

"That's right. And <u>you</u> were right. . . Somebody needed to tell the staff to stop slamming the doors at 6:00am . . . And I don't think they'll be doing it much in the future . . . But you needed to complain about it first to God."

"Complain to God?" Stone asked, puzzled. "Why complain to God about it? It wasn't his fault."

"He knew the perfect thing for you to do about it," Ezra smiled. "He knew what He wanted you to do about it. And he really could have stopped the banging."

"So God *wants* me to complain to him?"

"All complaining is complaining about God . . . and against God – even when you don't know it," Ezra winked and grinned. "It's saying, 'Hey, God, I don't like this. Why are things so bad? You could change things . . . God! You could make my life better. Why aren't you doing it? Why aren't you helping me?' . . . See? Whenever you're griping and moaning about anything, ultimately, you're complaining about God and against God," Ezra concluded.

"Never thought of it like that," Stone raised his brow and pondered.

"And He's all-powerful and He knows your troubles . . . And He really could change them . . . So, doesn't it make sense to do what King David did in that Psalm you read today and take your troubles to him?"

"I could see asking him for help," Stone said with a curious cock of his head, "but *complaining* to him? . . . Complaining to God about God – for something that isn't his fault? . . . That just doesn't seem right."

"He's not only all-powerful," Ezra grinned, "He is also all-*knowing*."

"Yes. But what does that have to do with complaining to him. Griping and moaning – like you say – to God."

"Any time you're angry," Ezra laughed, "at some level, you're ultimately angry at God . . . And He knew you were angry before you did. So, you might as well tell him about it . . . And get it worked out. He wants to hear from you – in all circumstances – about everything. And He knows what you need to do in every circumstance . . . And He will help you to do it. So . . . tell him about *everything – anything!* Even when you're angry . . . He <u>loves</u>

you . . . more than you can imagine – even when you're angry at him! And He wants to help – Even if you need to have it out with him first . . . and really let him have it. Believe it or not . . . He can take it – and still love you more than you can possibly imagine."

"So . . ." Stone said, wondering about all of this, that he had never heard – or imagined – before, "How should I have told the staff to stop banging at 6 o'clock in the blessed morning?!

"How in the blessed world should I know?!" Ezra boomed and cackled . . . "But it's not too late to take that complaint to God."

And Stone pulled out his index cards.

"I am now a dangerous Christian man," he wrote. "And that means that the devil will attack me . . . But I will take my complaints – and concerns and needs - to God because He defeated the devil and _all_ of my troubles."

"We're gonna take a break from the booklet, tomorrow," Ezra said, handing Hallelujah a C.D. "Listen to this instead."

"All right," Hallelujah quickly agreed. "But, y'know, I'm liking the booklet. Even looking forward to it."

"You'll like this, too," Ezra nodded with a nutty wink.

DAY NINE

THE MUSIC LILTED SLOWLY AND HAPPILY WITH SOMETHING like a 1950's western-swing style and a pleasing little who-knows-what. But the voice! What in the world? An old man croaking through 50 years of cigarettes and more than a few shots of Wild Turkey, every now and then – maybe Slivowitz or some good ol' Tennessee sour mash whiskey.

But that grizzled coyote-crooning did something to the words that took them beyond what you would read on a lyric sheet.

It was a love song called, "All the Time in the World" that had a simple, sweet and slow rhythm that was entirely at odds with the voice – at first.

Strange did not begin to describe this songs "uniqueness." But Stone couldn't help but listen; and the more he did, the more puzzled he became. Ezra had him reading a booklet of scriptures, which gave him some otherwise non-existent peace and which he was starting to understand - and even crave. It didn't make sense that Ezra would now give him a CD of an old man sweetly croaking out a love song that had nothing to do with God, the Bible, praying, or anything remotely related to the kind of faith in Jesus that Ezra had been teaching.

If it had been anybody other than Ezra Eliot Loleko, Stone would have figured that he was just giving him a break. But this was Ezra. And with Ezra, even taking a break meant that he was up to something.

Stone knew that there was something going on in that song. After all, Ezra had given it to him and that coyote-crooning said that there was more in those words than met the ear. He listened again. And a third time.

> I'll take all the time I need
> To praise your every deed.
> I know you know I come undone.
> And now there ain't no doubt.
> You're the permanent one.
> I got all the time in the world
> And the end has just begun.

By the time Stone met with Ezra, he had the words just about memorized. He wasn't trying to remember them, but they had been playing in his head all morning and into the middle of the afternoon. And he caught himself smiling like a person going through hell is not supposed to do.

"I don't have a clue why you gave me that song, crazy man," Stone poked at Ezra with a crooked smile – and a little light in his eyes that Ezra had not seen before. "But I can't get it out of my head."

"You've got more of a clue than you think you do, Mr. Livingstone," Ezra said wryly, flashing a raise of his brow.

"I hope."

"Yes, I know. You can't keep from hoping," Ezra grinned, intending something other than what Stone had meant.

"Why'd'ya give me a love song?"

"It's pretty simple."

"Yeah?"

"Yeah . . . You're living that love song."

"I ain't never been in love with nobody. And there isn't any woman whose gonna want a man whose locked in a crazy-coop . . . except, maybe, one of the nuts whose in here with me. Think of the disaster that would be."

Ezra laughed. "There are some beautiful women in here. And it might be good for you to be with somebody else who has been to the suburbs of hell."

"You know," Stone paused, "I think I'm doing better . . . I'm not dead. I'm not in hell. My brain has settled down some . . ."

"This song is going to show you how to get even better."

"I know there's something to it," Stone laughed and shook his head. "You're always up to something. You're not just wastin' time with this."

"Good, then, let's get at it! What's the first line?"

"I'll take all the time I need to praise your every deed."

"And _there's_ the key to understanding the whole song!" Ezra boomed.

"I'm not seein' it" Stone snapped. "A guy wants to get his girlfriend in bed, so he's lookin' for some con line to tell her how wonderful she is."

"Yep. That's what most in this world would think about that line," Ezra mused. "But I say the writer is using a metaphor that he knows most will miss."

"Why would he do that?"

"Because if he gave it to 'em straight, they'd tune it out and stone him . . . So, he does like Jesus sometimes did. He figures he'll just let him who has ears hear."

Stone smirked and rolled his eyes playfully. "What in the world does that mean?" he quipped.

"Those to whom God gives understanding will get it . . . But they might have to work at it. Spend some time with it – and even pray about it . . . if they care."

"So what's the line really mean," Stone asked, "in your most humble opinion?"

"You want me to just give it to you? You don't want the fun of workin' at it and spending time with it . . . and praying about it?"

"No. No, I don't want the fun of workin' at it."

"You will," Ezra grinned. "But since I'm teaching you how to do this . . . well, hmm . . . that's just as good of a reason _not_ to just give it to you."

Stone shook his head and rolled his eyes.

". . . But I will. Because I just love this," Ezra hooted and cackled. He sometimes just went delirious for a few seconds, which seemed to others like they might never end. Some enjoyed it. Some thought he was a pain. Ezra rollicked, either way.

"You get a kick out of yourself, don't you, crazy man," Stone marveled

"It's a trait that comes in handy," Ezra grinned, still hooting, all wide-eyed, silly and stupid – in a way that said he went about the world amazed at the simplest of things. Some would call him a goof – or worse – and did. But if one took a good look at Ezra, he would see that all that silliness was pure blessing bursting out of him. He couldn't contain it. Didn't want to. And it drew people to him – even when he would rather be alone. Deep down, even the ones who called him a goof – and worse – wanted what he had.

"So, stop cackling, already, and tell me what that line really means," Stone demanded with a cackle of his own.

"Listen to you laughin'"

Stone caught himself in mid-cackle.

"You didn't think you'd ever hear that again. You're changing, Hallelujah Livingstone."

Stone nodded and tried to agree. "Maybe . . . I guess so . . . I wasn't laughing much when I got here . . . and a good while before."

"'I'll take all the time I need,' the man says, 'to praise your every deed." Ezra sang in a croaking imitation of the song's author.

"Right!" Stone exclaimed, "He wants to get his girlfriend in bed."

"He ain't singin' to his girlfriend! . . . or about his girlfriend. She ain't worthy of the kind of praise he's talkin' about."

"O-o-o-h," Stone crooned, "So, that's what you're up to."

"That's right. He's singing to Jesus Christ. Every last word of that little ditty is a love song to the God-Man who saved his life. Saved him! From sin and death and satan."

"That song doesn't say a word about Jesus Christ or sin or death or satan or salvation," Stone protested.

"Every _word_ of it is a love song to Christ!"

"Why do you want me to know that?"

"Because giving your life to Jesus has saved _you_ from an eternity in hell." Ezra bellowed and beamed. "And you don't know it, but that laugh you let out a little while ago . . . that's the change that He has already begun in you. And praising him, like the man in this song praises him, will lift you up out of that pit you've been in . . . And it will lift you up every time you have to go through some kind of hell – big or small. And you will, from time-to-time have to go through different kinds of hell. But, so what? That small and temporary trouble can't compare with the glory that it is to be. The glory you will share with Christ. The glory that is already here for you in Him, as just a little foretaste of what is to come and blow you away."

The praise and glory of it all went past Stone.

"You still go through hell?" Stone asked disappointedly, finding it hard to imagine.

"Sure!" Ezra smiled. "We all do. But, for me, it ain't like it used to be. And it won't be for you, either."

"What makes you so sure?"

"'I'll take all the time I need,' Ezra croaked again, with a pseudo-gravel tone, "to praise your every deed. I know you know I come undone.' Look at that!," Ezra jumped. "He can't keep it in. He _must_ praise!" Ezra rambled, so excited that he couldn't possibly keep it in, either. "Man! . . . He doesn't even care about time. – just like he was in love with the most beautiful woman he had ever seen."

"Okay . . . He's pretty thrilled with God . . . with Jesus."

"Yeah! Yeah. Listen! *'I got all the time in the world and the end has just begun.'*"

"Yeah. So what's the big deal."

"Look, this guy has been a believer for a long earthly time. 30 years. And he says the end has just begun . . . His time <u>with God</u> has just begun! 30 years! . . . 30 years since He put his faith in Christ! And it's just *begun?* Yes! Yes! Yes!," Ezra could hardly contain himself. "Because 30 years ain't nothin' – not when this joy and peace and love is going to last beyond a lifetime . . . goin' bigger and better and closer throughout all eternity!"

And Ezra was singing out very loud again.

"When we've been there ten-thousand years, bright shining as the sun, we've no less days to sing God's praise. Praise! Praise, Hallelujah Livingstone. Praise! Than when we first begun."[32]

Stone laughed joyfully, catching Ezra's contagion. "That's not in the song, crazy man," he clowned.

"That's in Amazing Grace.[33] And it's 100% true. This love ain't goin' away, baby! This love will be there when you really do drop dead – and you'll know it more and more and more after that . . . all the ever-lovin' way through eternity!"

Stone just grinned and stared at the exploding joy that was Ezra Eliot Loleko. "No wonder," he thought, "that they locked this guy up." But he was coming to believe Ezra more and more. And he badly wanted what Ezra had.

"Look, look . . . look what comes next!" Ezra rocked on like a 6-and-a-half foot, blazing bundle of enthusiasm. He was so excited he could hardly get the words out.

> *"I tried their wine, their women, and their song.*
> *I know you know I never did belong.*
> *You knew all along, it was just a phase.*
> *I got all the time in the world*
> *To learn your ever-long-lovin' ways.*

"What's that mean?" Stone asked.

"What's it mean. Yes, yes . . . The world has messed him over!"

"What?"

"The wine, the women, and the song. That's the world. The neuro-depraved, soul-defiled-and-deceived world! Gone mad from sin. Gone mad _with_ sin!" Ezra exclaimed, " – and the world has messed him over. But it doesn't matter. He got caught up in it. He tasted the world's honey. Wine, women, and song. He sinned and it burned him. But Jesus paid the price for this man's sin. And, now, he has broken-up with the world and its sweet falsehoods. It was just a phase. They were just passin' by, caught him for a second, but, man, now, he's got all the time in the world!"

"What difference does the time make?" Stone laughed. "So, he's got all the time in the world?"

"C'mon, man. His time with Jesus has just begun! He's gonna be basking in God's love – learnin' all about it - forever. Forever! . . . You know what that means? . . ."

"A long time." Stone said.

"It means time don't mean nothin'!"

"You're seeing all that in those few words that don't say anything about God?" Stone gave a crooked, half-believing smile.

"You better believe it! It's true," Ezra boomed and beamed. "And even if that isn't what the writer/singer means . . . I see it. It's there . . . and it's true . . . and it's wonderful!

"Now-listen-to-this-next-line," Ezra speeded in one word – and cackled and spit and laughed with a thousand watts. "Man! It just gets better'n'better. Listen."

> _"Happy the man whose seen what I've seen,_
> _Near enough to the fire to be burned."_

"What in the world is that all about?!" Ezra shrieked, knowing full-well exactly what he thought about those lines.

Ezra was too excited to give Stone a chance to speak. Too

excited to even wonder whether Stone wanted to speak. It was all bursting out of his chest like he couldn't contain it if he tried. And he had no desire to try.

"His heart is cheerful. He never fears anything . . . What? He doesn't fear anything even though he's been near enough to the fire to be burned? . . . No! No!" Ezra answered his own rhetorical question. "_Because_ he's been near enough to the fire to be burned. That's why he doesn't fear. He has seen the worst the world has to offer . . . And he has seen God blow it away! Don't you see?"

Stone tried to respond, but Ezra was too fast.

"Don't you see?" Ezra repeated. "That's _why_ he's praising God right from the first words of the song. He has seen God blow away the worst that the world has to offer – well . . . that's one of the reasons he's praising God. There's so many! Ha!" the crazy man cackled. "So many!"

He was going full throttle and it was a wonder to behold. Stone had questions, but they could wait. His heart was leaping at Ezra's mad-wild joy and he just wanted to listen and stare, hoping that if he stayed close, he might get infected. And he already was.

Ezra plowed onward. "He's seen God blow away the worst of the world – near to the fire, right outside of hell – just like you, Hallelujah Livingstone! And he knows. He knows!"

"Knows what?!" Stone quickly managed to interrupt.

"That as long as he stays close to God – and praises, and gets closer – God will blow away anything stupid enough to come against him. Because he is a brother of Christ – a child of God – and when anything comes against him, it comes against Jesus, too. And God blows it away! Yeah-Yeah-Yeah!" Ezra sang out loud. "She loves you, yeah-yeah-yeah!" he wailed and howled and flopped around.

Stone was eager for more. "Next line! What's that?" he shouted over Ezra's madness, fearing that the nurses, aides, and security might break in on the uproar at any minute. But it _was_ a nuthouse.

The staff was used to "uproar" and only broke in when uproar was about to turn to kickin' and swingin'.

"The next line? Oh . . . Yes! Yes! The next line." Ezra careened.

"Near enough o the fire to be burned – yeah. You're shoutin' somethin'. I ain't afraid-a-nothin'.I saw the whole world tossed and turned."

"You know," Ezra mused, "here's the funny thing. I'm not sure this whole verse – the fire and bein' happy and never fearing and seeing the whole world tossed and turned?" he spun his eyes and twisted his grin. "I'm not sure it's the singer talkin' to God or God talkin' to the singer."

"Yeah?" Stone cocked his head and squinted, "So, what do you do with that?"

"Doesn't matter!" Ezra yelped. "It's great either way!"

"How?"

Well, look at this. You know God doesn't have to be in any hurry. He's got all the time in the world to accomplish what He wants to accomplish. He invented "Time" – *and* the world. And He sure as hell – and there sure is a hell – He sure ain't afraid of anybody shoutin' and getting angry at Him . . . C'mon, man. Afraid?! He's conquered all evil! He's crushed satan with the Cross of Christ. And in the end He's going to lock him in a lake of eternal fire."

"And how does this verse work if it's the singer talkin'?" Stone asked excitedly; wanting to know.

"The singer's God has crushed all evil! Crushed satan! Conquered death and jumped right up out of the grave. His God is a *b-a-a-a-d* man! What does the singer have to fear? . . . Anything comes against him . . . he can take up the Name of his Commander-in-Chief and say, 'In Jesus Name, I command you satan . . . I *command* you – and all your demons and anything else that comes against me . . . I *command* you, in Jesus Name, depression, fear, anxiety, pain, illness, terror . . . be gone from me! My Jesus rebukes you. Now, go to hell, where you belong!"

Stone sat amazed. "That's some pretty powerful stuff."

"You're rippin' right it is," Ezra laughed.

"I've never heard anything like that."

"It's all true," Ezra declared "and you can do it, too – just like me and the singer."

Stone shook his head. "I wouldn't bet on that."

"You might not have the guts to do it - yet," Ezra popped in a fully sincere and entirely playful manner that brought a hard – and just as playful – sneer from Stone. "But the Power to do it is in you – right now."

"Crazy man, how do you figure that I have the power to _command_ – as you say – satan?"

"Man, do you not understand what happened when you took on Jesus Christ as your Lord and Savior?! . . . He gave you authority – more authority – His authority! More than you know," Ezra roared.

"I have authority?" Stone grinned with almost complete doubt. "I have authority to command satan? You have blown a fuse, Crazy man."

"So what? I'm crazy," Ezra clowned, "Doesn't change the fact that you have authority to command satan. But you don't do it on your own. On your own you are no match for the devil."

"That," Stone laughed, "I can agree with."

"You stand in the Power of the Cross and Resurrection of Christ, Hallelujah!" Ezra boomed. "And it's Christ's authority that you declare against the devil – and depression and fear and anxiety and terror – and the devil sprints straight back to hell where he belongs . . . But don't get lazy! He'll wait for another chance. And you'll need to be ready to throw another haymaker in the Name of your Commander-in-Chief, Jesus Christ."

"How do I stay ready?"

"Do what you've been doing. Get closer and closer to God. To

Jesus. To the Holy Spirit. Pray. Read His Word. And praise, praise, praise!"

"Next line," Stone demanded.

> *Anna-Nicole and Madonna,*
> *Pizza, Pasta, Lasagna,*
> *I'm thinkin' bout a virgin queen.*
> *I got all the time in the world*
> *And, you know, I think you know what I mean."*

"That's nuts!" Stone smirked playfully. "Anna-Nicole and Madonna? You're gonna tell me that's all about God, right?!"

"It's a whole lot like that second verse when he never did belong with the wine, the women, and the song of the world . . . Pizza, pasta, lasagna, baby! He's done with buffoonery. He's not fallin' for the world's Anna-Nicoles and Madonnas. He's thinkin' bout a virgin queen. You know, the mother of our Lord. And our singer is going to spend some time fixing his mind on her amazing example of faith – and turn away from the scarlet whore of the world and its opposition to every Godly thing."

"Two more verses," Stone said.

"Yes! Let's go. This is good."

"You say that about all of them."

"Yes! Yes! And they are!" Ezra revved.

> *They moan and they complain.*
> *Might as well go insane.*
> *They work and they work and they work.*
> *Workin' to bleed themself to death.*
> *Lyin' eyes Luc?*
> *What's he gonna do?*
> *I'll stomp his corpse*
> *And give him smoke for breath.*

"Yeah! This is God speaking again," Ezra exclaimed, "Or maybe the singer."

"And what are either of them saying?" Stone asked, shaking his head at the joyfully unbridled lunatic in front of him - who was making more sense than anybody Stone had ever heard speak.

"The unbelievers are moanin' and comlainin'. Just like they have from the dawn of time . . . Denying God. Denying that He exists . . . Creating their own false gods, in their own images and likenesses . . . But they're dying in their own blood because they have rejected Christ . . . See, we all pay in blood for our sins. But we - the believers — we pay with the blood Jesus shed at the Cross . . . The unbelievers, because they've rejected Christ's blood . . . they gotta pay with their own — and an eternity in hell . . . Unless they get things figured out and give their lives to Christ before they drop dead. Just like you did, my brother – in Christ . . . and madness!"

"Whose this Lyin' Eyes Luc," Stone asked. "Sounds goofy."

"Who do you think it is," Ezra asked, with no intention of waiting for an answer. "Satan! . . . And what does God say about him? . . . I'll stomp his cursed corpse . . . You know what I think is so wonderful about that?"

"O-o-o-h, I'll bet it's something wild," Stone crooned about half as crazily as Ezra. "And I've got no doubt that you're gonna tell me."

"It says 'his corpse.' Satan's corpse!"

"Yeah? . . . So?"

"His *corpse*, man!" Ezra howled. "Satan's corpse. He's already as good as dead! . . . And God's sayin' 'I ain't worried about that fool – and you shouldn't be, either, because I'll stomp his dirty, dead backside into dust!'"

Stone laughed harder, louder, and longer than he had in what seemed like a full year. He was cackling just about like Ezra. "You really think," he choked with laughter, "You really think God would say, 'I'll stomp his *dirty, dead backside* into dust?'"

"I think He might even put it a little rougher than that!" Ezra blasted. "God ain't the sissy the heathen world makes Him out to be. He's WILD, man! The Bible says He's a warrior! . . . He's gonna tell it like it is. No sugar-coated, soft-boiled buffoonery . . . Man, I'm sick of that sissy image of God – that even some churches have. My God is a <u>WARRIOR</u>! . . . He *Will* drag the devil's dirty, dead backside through the mud and He isn't going to be shy about saying so! In plain English . . . or any other plain vernacular – and He ain't gonna be shy about doing it."

What's this line about givin' his corpse "smoke for breath?" Stone asked.

Ezra grinned a fiendishly Godly grin. "That ain't pure, enviro-friendly oxygen they're swallowin' in hell!"

"Hallelujah!" Stone roared like he was ready to join Ezra in the army of God.

"Next verse!" Stone boldly commanded.

"Last verse," Ezra fired back.

Crunch-time's come crackin' round the bend
Clear 'n' closer than it's ever been
I didn't think you cared
Could not believe you could be true.
I got all the time in the world
And I'm gonna spend it with you.

Ezra grinned coyly. "Why don't you take a shot at this one, Livingstone. I think you can come up with something good – and right in line with the Word of God that you've been reading."

"Oh you do?" Stone winked and mused.

"Sure," Ezra confidently encouraged, "You've been studying scripture. You've got the Holy Spirit living in you, now, to give you knowledge and understanding. And you've got me right here in front of you - in case you get too far out of whack."

"Yeah . . ." Stone playfully hesitated. "But how am I supposed to know what the man who wrote this song meant by those lines."

"I don't _know_ what he meant!" Ezra said with his pseudo-lunatic beam.

"What?!" Stone yelped, astounded. "So, what have we been doing here?! . . . I thought you were _telling_ me what he meant."

"I don't need to know what _he_ meant. It's not scripture. He's just a man . . . I don't need to know what he meant, like I need to know what God means in the Bible," Ezra explained. "I can interpret the man's song any way I want to – can't do that with scripture - and I see Jesus in the song. So, why not? . . . I haven't given an unbiblical interpretation . . . and I do believe that the man who wrote the song is a full-blooded, Bible-believing, hard-core Christian . . . an Outlaw Christian, I like to call it."

"An Outlaw Christian? What's that?"

"Not now," Ezra said, putting his hands up as a way of saying 'Stop.'

"But he's never told you what the song means – and you've never read anything about what he says the song means."

"Nope," Ezra replied with a goofy grin. "And I don't need to know what he means. Now you take a shot at it."

"Do I have a choice?" Stone laughed.

"Only if you want to break your commitment to follow my program for How to Go through Hell."

"Alright!" Stone nodded powerfully, with a shiny grin, suddenly bursting with confidence. "Lucky for me that I think this one's pretty easy.

"That ain't luck!" Ezra growled a friendly admonishment. "That's the Holy Spirit."

"Yes! Yes! Yes!" Stone boomed, gleefully imitating Ezra's patented line. "Here goes."

> _Crunch-time's come crackin' round the been_
> _Clear 'n' closer than it's ever been_
> _I didn't think you cared_
> _Couldn't believe you could be true._

I got all the time in the world
And I'm gonna spend it with you.

"We're closer to the end of time than ever before," Stone laughed at his own eminently obvious statement. "And people need to make their choice – just like I did. Surrender – submit! Or keep fighting futilely against God."

"Yes! Yes! Yes!" Ezra clowned. "Sounds good. Onward!"

"I didn't think you cared. Couldn't believe you could be true"... He was intrigued when he first found out about Jesus, but he didn't think it could all be true. He doubted ... Now? Well ... *"I got all the time in the world"*... His new life has just begun – and he's gonna spend every minute, now and on through eternity with Jesus."

"There you go! I love it." Ezra exclaimed. "Now ... would any of that be any less true if the singer was actually talking the whole time about a woman – he just wanted in the sack?"

Stone laughed out loud. "Who is this singer, anyway? Who wrote the song?"

"Ain't talkin'," Ezra grinned.

"You're not gonna tell me who wrote the song?"

Ezra shrugged.

Later that day, Stone wrote this in his notebook:

"Praise God! He deserves it – always – just because He's God. *I'll take all the time I need to praise your every deed!* My praise brings God joy. And God's joy is my strength.

"Praise God! It brings me into His Presence - where people and circumstances can't help but be transformed!"

DAY TEN

"DO NOT BE WORRIED AND UPSET," JESUS TOLD THEM.
"Believe in God and believe also in me. There are many rooms in my Father's house, and I am going to prepare a place for you. I would not tell you this if it were not so. And after I go and prepare a place for you, I will come and take you back to myself, so that you will be where I am. You know the way that leads to the place where I am going."[34]

"You ever hear the song 'Don't Worry. Be Happy?'[35] Stone asked Ezra.

"Yeah. Bobby McFerrin. Late 80's," Ezra twisted a crooked-goofy grin. "Robin Williams was in the video."

"I hate that song," Stone blasted.

"Me, too," Ezra kept grinning.

"You do? Why?" Stone asked, surprised. "Why would you hate a song that tells you not to worry? Just be happy? That sounds like it's right up your alley."

"It's buffoon-sense."

"Yes-it-is," Stone snapped in one word. "But I'm surprised that you would think so. I can't picture you worrying about anything."

"I don't. But you're lookin' at the 43-year-old version of Ezra Eliot Loleko."

"You used to worry."

"When I was a little older than you, I was a mess . . . When that song came out I was going through my own hell – and didn't know how to get out. I worried about everything . . . and I _hated_ that song."

"You went through hell?"

"That's why I'm here."

"In a psych ward? You're not going through hell now."

"No. And my hell wasn't like yours. People go through all kinds of hell. Brain cancer. Drugs. Alcohol. The death of a child. Sex abuse . . . But that's not it. I'm not here in front of you because I'm going through hell now . . . I'm not . . . I'm here in front of you because I went through hell a good while ago, and it taught me how to teach you to go through hell. And get through hell . . . And look back and call it a blessing . . . Y'see, there's all kinds of hell, but they've all got the same way out."

"So, why do you still hate that song?" Stone asked. "You don't worry, now, and you look and sound like the happiest person I have ever seen or heard."

"I still hate that song because it's still buffoon-sense."

"You know why I hate that song?" Stone growled through grit teeth. "Because it sounds right . . . It sounds like exactly what I should be doing . . . And I couldn't . . . And that blaring song was laughing in my face."

"That's right . . . and it's buffoon-sense."

"Tell me about it."

"Sure," Ezra beamed. "It sounds great. Just stop worrying, put every bad thing aside, turn that frown upside-down and just become a happy idiot, right?"

"That's what it sounds like to me, but it was a big hit and people seem to love it."

"Y-e-e-e-s," Ezra crazy-crooned. "People love buffoon-sense

when it sounds clever and calming and happy. And they want to do it. And they try to do it . . . They even pretend to believe that they are doing it . . . But it's buffoon-sense."

"Yes! Yes! Yes!" Stone suddenly beamed, as if he were Ezra, which caught Ezra a little by pleased surprise. "And, you know," Stone happily carried on, "Just a few days ago, I would have thought today's verse from your little plan was the same kind of buffoon-sensed nit-wittery."

"Oh?" Ezra laughed, "Sounds like you might be on to something."

"Indeed!" Stone boomed. "Just a few days ago, I would have read, *'Don't be worried and upset, Jesus told them,'*[36] and I would have sailed your little booklet across the room and growled out everything I have to worry about."

"Sounds like something's changed," Ezra flashed a mischievous, loony-eyed grin.

"I would have thrown that booklet and seethed, 'Don't be worried and upset?! . . . Buffoon-Sense! . . . I'm out of work. I've got $60,000 in school loans that are about to default. And what'd I get out of that? A lousy degree in Political Science that won't get me a job . . . I lost – quit! - the best chance I'll ever have – baseball. I don't even have my own pot to pee in. And, now, to top it all off, I'm locked in a nuthouse! . . . And you, Jesus, have the nerve to tell me not to be worried and upset?! Whose the nut here, Jesus?' Stone accurately surmised. "That's what I would have done – if I had read that verse just a few days ago."

"All true," said Ezra, with his loony-eyed twinkle," And just a few days ago you _would_ have said that . . . but not now, I wonder . . ."

"No. Not now," Stone declared. "That buffoon-sense song said, 'Don't worry. Be happy' and stopped right there."

"Yes."

"Jesus didn't stop there. He didn't stop with *'Don't be worried and upset.'*[37] I would not have seen that just a few days ago. Jesus – unlike the buffoon-sense nut-wittery of our day, told us how to do it! . . . He showed us how not to be worried and upset . . . He _knew_ – just like we do – that it was futile to try to just 'Not worry and Be Happy.' That it was useless – even self-defeating – to even think that we could just decide to stop worrying and simply choose to be happy . . . I tried . . . And it is, indeed, buffoonery . . . Jesus gave us a way to stop worrying and being upset!"

"Jesus, Mr. Livingstone," said Ezra, "gave us _the_ way to stop worrying and being upset."

"I'll go you one further, Mr. Loleko," Stone charged, "Jesus is _the way_ to stop worrying and being upset."

"Yes! Yes! Yes!" Ezra exulted.

"Look at what He said," Stone raved.

"Sounds like a good idea."

"Do not be worried and upset,"[38] Stone cackled and grinned, throwing a triumphant fist in the air and popping his eyes goofily - exuberantly – wide open. _Believe in God and believe also in me,"_[39] . . . _That_ is what He said."

"And why did He say it?" Ezra leadingly asked."

"Because He _knew_ what He was doing . . . And He _knew_ that He was going to prepare a place for _me_! Don't you see, Ezra?" Stone exclaimed, as if he were teaching Ezra and Ezra was again learning this for the first time. _"And He says that He will come and take me – evil, sinner _me_ – back to him."_ And I will be where He is . . . He ain't no liar, Ezra. Either what He says is true or He's a liar . . . or . . . a full-blown _lunatic_ – bigger than this place has ever seen before. But He's the Lord! . . . It is true. And if my end is heaven – an eternity in paradise greater than anything I could imagine – then, no matter how bad things are here, no matter how bad they might get, then I have _Nothing_ to worry about. Nothing, man! I'm going to heaven. And Jesus . . . Jesus! . . . is the way."

"Yep," Ezra easily declared. "And, you know what? You didn't figure this out for yourself."

"You gave me a lot of it. You set me on the road," Stone acknowledged. "But I did make some pretty big conclusions on my own."

"You did a whole lot more than draw conclusions," Ezra rampantly cackled for joy.

"Whaddaya mean?" Stone asked.

"You, Mr. Hallelujah . . . listened . . . The Holy Spirit spoke. And you listened! . . . And believed . . . He opened this scripture to your mind – to your spirit . . . And He will keep doing it! . . . Just listen – and ask for everything you need to be able to do what He says."

Stone quickly – boldly – moved toward Ezra and hugged him – hard – around the neck and chest, leaning his chin on Ezra's shoulder – cheek against cheek – and whispered . . . "Thank you . . . my friend."

And Ezra slapped him a hearty pat on the back and asked, "You ever consider the initials of Buffoon Sense?"

DAY ELEVEN

STONE COULD NOT STOP CRYING. HE SIGHED AND SIGHED
again and inhaled deeply, but the dry lump in his throat would not
go away. A chill shivered down the back of his neck and shook his
shoulders . . . He smiled and rubbed his face and shook . . . and
went back, sobbing, to the passage he had just read.

The Lord is my shepherd;
I have everything I need.
He lets me rest in fields of green grass
 and leads me to quiet pools of fresh water.
He gives me new strength.
He guides me in the right paths,
 as He has promised.
Even if I go through the deepest darkness,
 I will not be afraid, Lord,
 for you are with me.
Your shepherd's rod and staff protect me.

You prepare a banquet for me,
 where all my enemies can see me;

you welcome me as an honored guest
and fill my cup to the brim.
I know that your goodness and
love will be with me all my life;
and your house will be my
home as long as I live.[40]

Stone's lips quivered and the tears kept coming and he knew that he looked like a big baby. And he laughed out loud. The 6-foot-6-inch, blubbering, big baby, 225-pound professional pitcher no longer cared how crazy he might look. Joy was billowing up in him and bursting out of him in tears of mad, cackling laughter. And in his <u>*spirit*</u>, he was back on that pitcher's mound in Hickory, North Carolina and hugging – with all his mighty strength – that 22-year-old closer whose mind and soul were splitting in two. And Stone yelled into his ear, "You made it, man! . . . You made it! . . . I love you! . . . <u>God</u> (!) loves you!"

And Stone grabbed that young pitcher by the shoulders – with every eye in the stadium on him – and he shook him and smiled and roared with joy. "You have been through the *deepest* darkness! – just outside the gates of Hell! . . . And you made it, man! You made it out!"

"Do not be afraid," Stone wildly boomed to his minor league closer friend, "The <u>Lord</u> is with you – now! Even now – when you are far from him . . . He is coming after you. The <u>Lord</u> is *fighting* for you! And He will *always* be with you . . . Always! . . . You have *everything* you need . . . Everything! . . . The Lord knows what you need – even before you ask . . . . And He <u>*will*</u> give it to you. He will do it. <u>He</u> will do it!"

"Yes! Yes! Yes!" Ezra blasted as he approached the mound, with the crowd looking on. "And the Lord will not just *give* you everything you need . . . The Lord <u>*IS*</u> everything you need!"

And the 26-year-old Stone grinned, while the 22-year-old minor-leaguer stared in amazement.

And Ezra boomed for joy, "You have need of only one thing, Hallelujah Livingtone!" . . . "And you have chosen that <u>one</u> right thing. <u>You!</u> Hallelujah, have chosen the better part. And <u>it</u> . . . <u>will</u> . . . <u>NOT</u> . . . be taken from you!"[41]

And the 22-year-old Stone and the 26-year-old Hallelujah cried out loud – together . . . tears of joy.

DAY TWELVE

AS EZRA OPENED THE DOOR TO ENTER STONE'S ROOM, A
broad nurse filled the threshold and Ezra stepped aside.

"You don't have to hold the door because I'm a woman," the
nurse sternly admonished.

And Ezra didn't miss a beat.

"I'm not holding the door because you're a woman," he fiendishly
sparkled.

"Hmmph," the nurse snorted.

"I'm holding it because of your age."

The nurse pushed past without another word and Stone grinned
just as fiendishly as Ezra. "I wonder whether she could get by with
a little help from my friends?" he goofily crooned."

"Which ones?" Ezra laughed.

"Take your pick . . . Seroquel? . . . Lamotragine? . . . Welbutrin?"

"Benadryl," Ezra shot back, "She might just need some sleep."

"Neurontin! That'll put her out for 8 to 10 hours," Stone ruefully
laughed, knowing that, just a few days ago, the only peace he
thought he would ever get was a few hours of chemically induced
sleep. "Y'know, Ezra, we all got troubles . . . who knows what hell

might be going on in her life?" he said with a new, compassionate recognition that he wasn't in this capsized boat alone.

"Yeeaah," Ezra drawled, "Funny you should mention that."

"Oh?" Stone smiled knowingly. "Why am I not surprised that you're already up to something?"

"Can't help it. You led me smack into that little scripture passage that you read today . . . What was it again?"

"You know darn well what it was." Stone snapped playfully.

"Yeah, but, y'know, somehow, I really need to hear it from you." Ezra grinned.

And Stone, to his own surprise, already had it memorized.

"What we are teaching you now is the Lord's teaching: we who are alive on the day the Lord comes will not go ahead of those who have died. There will be the shout of command, the archangel's voice, the sound of God's trumpet, and the Lord himself will come down from heaven. Those who have died believing in Christ will rise to life first; then we who are living at that time will be gathered up along with them in the clouds to meet the Lord in the air. And so we will always be with the Lord. So then, encourage one another with these words."[42]

Ezra didn't ask Stone what he thought of that passage. He didn't ask him what God might be telling him with those words. Ezra knew what God's message was for Stone – and that he had been sent to deliver it.

"There's one more thing you need to do," Ezra instructed.

"Sell all I have and give it to the poor?" Stone grinned. "There ain't much."

Ezra rolled his eyes, smirked playfully, and shook his head – much the same as Stone had frequently done when Ezra said something screwy.

"You have to give," Ezra said, "but it's something in which you are abundantly rich."

Stone turned serious. He didn't think there was anything in

which he was 'abundantly rich' – except maybe a hair-trigger temper.

"When people talk to you about their weaknesses, brother Livingstone – and they will – easily, because they'll see this in you," Ezra declared, "When they talk to you about their weaknesses, you are going to see their strengths . . . And it won't be a whole lot of work for you. You will be eager . . . joyful (!) to tell them about their strengths."

"Sounds like a good thing to do," Stone nodded quizzically and shrugged, "But you're not saying that I should do it. You're saying that I *will*. You sound certain . . . like you *know* it."

"I am . . . And I do."

"Well, I haven't done much of that kind of thing lately . . . too knotted up in my own weakness. But I did do that," Stone said wistfully, "with my teammates in Hickory . . . and even Vanderbilt – when I wasn't too hungover."

"It's going to be different now," Ezra emphatically insisted.

"Well, yeah . . . I'll be sober . . . But that's not what you're talking about . . . and how do you know this about me, anyway?"

"You know that when we become Christians," Ezra said, "when we give our lives to Christ, let him be our Lord and Leader – He sends the Holy Spirit to dwell in us."

"Yes. I know."

"Well, He also gives us a ministry. He calls us to do something for him."

"Uh-oh." Stone exclaimed, "Sounds like you're getting ready to drop another bomb on me."

"Be not afraid!" Ezra demanded. "The Holy Spirit that Jesus sent to dwell in you – _He_ will equip you for that ministry. _He_ will be working in you – and not just in you, but through you to accomplish the work Jesus calls you to do. The work He sends you to do."

"How?"

"He gives each of us – Christians – specific, Spirit-filled gifts,"

Ezra professed. "A lot of people – Christians – don't know the gifts he has given them . . . or their tremendous power . . . but they are there, waiting, inside of their spirit – with the Person of the Holy Spirit."

Stone didn't know what to say, so, he wisely didn't say anything.

"You're gift, Hallelujah Livingstone, is encouragement! And you are *'abundantly rich'* in it."

"Well, uh, like I said," Stone stammered with surprise and uncertainty, "I did something like that – in Hickory – but not lately."

"Not lately?!" Ezra shrieked. "Really? . . . What do you think you were doing when you spoke to the Hickory Hillcats' closer, Hallelujah Livingstone, on the pitcher's mound yesterday?"

"Talkin' to myself . . . like any other nut," Stone laughed.

"You were using your gift of encouragement!" Ezra emphatically declared. "And you are going to use it many more times to come."

"Okay. Why not?" Stone nodded. "I did it in Hickory and Vanderbilt – just pickin' up my teammates."

"Not like this, brother!" Ezra boomingly belly-laughed. "And not like other people . . . With you, Hallelujah, there will be _power_!"

Stone liked the sound of that – _power_! But the thought knocked him back a bit. "Who . . . am I---" he wavered haltingly.

"You, Livingstone!" Ezra blasted and barreled on. "You are a dangerous Christian man, *filled* with the Holy Spirit of God! *Filled* . . . to overflowing!"

Stone wept.

"Listen, my brother," Ezra gently, firmly instructed. "Other people try to give a struggling soul a pat on the back . . . a little advice, a passing good wish. Not you! . . . The Holy Spirit is going to take charge. The Holy Spirit is going to move in _power_ – to give God's Encouragment through you!"

"Wow," Stone whispered with childlike awe – and acceptance.

"Yeah," Ezra smiled and nodded firmly. "Wow."

"What do I have to do?" Stone asked innocently.

"Keep on getting closer to Jesus!" Ezra enthused. "And let the Holy Spirit do his work in you and through you – and enjoy him to the fullest! . . . Know his power. Know his strength – strengthening you. And encouraging _you_ through it all . . . *Equipping* you!"

Stone was shaken. He trembled. "H-how do you know this?"

"Remember, now, Livingstone . . . You ain't the only one who got a gift from the Holy Spirit," Ezra winked. "He lets me know things."

DAY THIRTEEN

THE UNMISTAKABLE BOOM OF EZRA ELIOT LOLEKO bellowed through the hallways.

"I am going peacefully!" he roared. "But I am first going to speak . . . one more word to these people . . . before I go – and you will NOT be able to stop me."

Stone burst through the door of his room and into the hallway. "Ezra!" he demanded, "What's going on?"

Two male aides and three burly-fat security guards surrounded the fiery giant Loleko. They had not let his 43 years fool them into thinking that his strength had been weakened in the least by age. And they were right. He wasn't going anywhere just yet and they were wisely disinclined to force him.

"Hallelujah Livingstone!" Ezra boomed and beamed. "It looks, my brother, like my work here is just about finished," he said with a wave around the hall – and smiled.

Stone was stunned. Patients were standing just outside half of the doors on that floor, waiting to hear what Ezra had to say. A rarely seen nurse had come out from behind the unit station. She trembled, eagerly – expectantly.

Ezra turned to the two aides and three guards surrounding

him. "I'm going to speak to Mr. Livingstone privately," he said, without any hint of asking permission. He walked toward Stone without waiting for a response and the aides and guards let him go.

"Ezra . . . what is this?" Stone asked quietly.

"I'm being transferred to the State Psychiatric Hospital at Camp Hill."

Stone's jaw dropped and his eyes popped wide open.

"You're the healthiest person in this place, Ezra. Doctors, nurses, counselors, bloodhounds, and aides included," Stone snapped loud enough for half the hall to hear.

"You remember yesterday's scripture?" Ezra stated, blowing right past Stone's compliment.

"Yes. Of course!"

"This is what you must write on your index card."

Stone grinned. "I thought I got to decide what to write on _my_ index cards."

"Not today. And as you can see," Ezra grinned, "I have no time for a debate. Write this . . . _'I will encourage others with these words. The Word of God. And I will give them the plan that Ezra gave me – with whatever scriptures God chooses for them.'_ Do you understand this, Stone?" he said firmly.

"Yes."

"You must do this. You cannot keep this to yourself. The Word of God. The Plan. What God has done for you – and in you – He wants to also do _through_ you."

Stone suddenly choked back a tear and felt a chill go down his neck and shiver his shoulders.

"You will always have the love and the peace and the joy of God with you, Stone . . . as long as you stay close to Jesus. But you cannot hoard it. It will only grow in you if you share it. And these people – and many others – need it. Desperately."

"I know. I must. I will," Stone said resolutely, looking firmly into Ezra's eyes. "But why are you saying this again. You told me yesterday. Do you think I don't remember what you say?"

"Hallelujah," Ezra said strongly, "You kept your commitment to read the scriptures. To follow the Plan. You are a man who keeps his commitments . . . Will you make this commitment; to encourage others with the Word of God and to give this Plan to those who are going through hell?"

Stone had many questions – and doubts – when he made his first commitment to Ezra; to follow the Plan. He did not hesitate this time. "Yes! I will!" he boldly declared. "I commit myself to encouraging others. To encouraging others with the Word of God. I will give the plan to people who are going through hell."

"You'll need to discuss and explain scriptures to them," Ezra sincerely cautioned, "As I did with you . . . Will you do that?"

"Yes," Stone quickly replied, "But I don't know the scriptures like you do."

"No, you don't," Ezra humbly acknowledged, "Not yet. But you will learn . . . and you don't have to wait . . . You can already share what you have now. And as you read the rest of the Bible, the Holy Spirit will give you understanding. And you will share more . . . And know more. And learn more in the very act of sharing the Word of God."

"I will do it," Stone said. "I must do it . . . I don't think I could keep myself from sharing the Word of God after what has happened to me – what God has done for me! It would burst out of my chest if I kept my mouth shut."

Ezra nodded firmly, looking directly into Stone's face, and wrapped his arms around him. And the two giants embraced – tightly – for a moment long enough to make the many - who were all still intensely watching and waiting – uncomfortable.

As the two men parted, Stone whispered, "You've been giving the Plan to all of these people, haven't you?"

"There are many kinds of hell that people go through, Stone. Cancer, addiction, the loss of a child, financial ruin, homelessness, divorce, prison, and many more. I share different parts of scripture wherever, however, and to whomever God directs. And the Holy Spirit works The Plan as He sees fit . . . And He uses me as He sees fit."

"And He'll use me as He sees fit,"Stone joyfully stated - and asked at the same time.

"Yes." Ezra declared. "As long as you let him."

"How will I know that I am doing what He wants me to do? That I am letting him use me as He sees fit?"

Ezra grinned goofily. "Love. Joy. Peace. Patience. Goodness. Kindness. Gentleness. Faithfulness. And Self-Control."

"The fruits of the Holy Spirit," Stone nodded.

"Yes . . . But remember, they are the *fruits* of <u>His</u> work in you. They are products of the work that <u>He</u> is doing in you."

"And I'll see those things in me – love, joy, peace, patience . . ." Stone asked, "if I'm letting the Holy Spirit use me as He sees fit?"

But Ezra turned to the rest of the patients, aides, nurses, and guards, who were still waiting for him because, before speaking with Stone, he had roared that – without any doubt – he was going to speak one more word to them. And they knew that Ezra would do what he said he was going to do.

Stone counted fifteen people standing in the hall waiting to receive what Ezra had to say. There were many others, whom Stone could not see, standing in their rooms or sitting in their chairs with their doors open, listening expectantly.

Ezra beamed and somehow seemed to be smiling at each person, individually, at the same time. His overwhelming presence calmly – humbly – filled the hallway, end to end.

"May you *always* be joyful in your union with the Lord,"[43] Ezra boomed into every corner of the long psych-ward unit. "I say it again: rejoice![44]

"Show a gentle attitude toward everyone,"[45] he exultingly – exuberantly – continued. "The Lord is coming soon. Don't worry about anything,"[46] he paused and let that sink in . . . "Don't worry about anything . . . but in all your prayers ask God for what you need, always asking with a thankful heart. And God's peace, which is far beyond human understanding . . ."[76] he paused again . . . "And <u>God's peace</u> – which is <u>far beyond <i>human understanding</i></u> – will keep your hearts and minds safe in union with Christ Jesus."[48]

"In conclusion, my brothers, fill your minds with those things that are good and that deserve praise: things that are true, noble, right, pure, lovely, and honorable. Put into practice what you learned from me, both from my words and from my actions. And the God who gives us peace . . . <u>will</u> be with <u>you</u>."[49]

And the rarely seen nurse who had come out from behind the unit station, trembling eagerly and expectantly, powerfully boomed, "Phillippians! Chapter 4. Verses 4 through 9."

"Yes! Yes!" Ezra exclaimed. "Now, if you have any questions," Ezra said to everyone – and pointed at Stone, "Barnabas over here is fully qualified to help you."

Ezra turned to the guards, whom he had not noticed losing their patience, and said, "Okay. I'm ready." But they were stopped dead by the gravelly cry of a broken-down schizophrenic man, who lovingly croaked, "There's a lot of <i>Buffoon Sense</i> in this place, Ezra Eliot Loleko . . . but we never got that from you . . . You will be missed."

As the guards and aides led him down the hallway; out the formerly banging, metal double-doors; and onto the ambulance that would take him to the State Psychiatric Institution at Camp Hill, the broad, beaming smile never left Ezra's face.

Stone returned to his room and eagerly read that day's scripture:

With great power the apostles gave witness to the resurrection of the Lord Jesus, and God poured rich blessings on them all. There was no one in the group who was in need. Those who owned fields or houses would sell them, bring the money received from the sale, and turn it over to the apostles; and the money was distributed according to the needs of the people.

And so it was that Joseph, a Levite born in Cyprus, whom the apostles called Barnabas (which means "One who Encourages"), sold a field he owned, brought the money, and turned it over to the apostles. [50]

DAY FOURTEEN

THERE WAS NO TELLING WHAT EZRA MIGHT BE GOING through in a state psych hospital. And Stone arose the following morning with the worst possibilities rushing through his brain. Seclusion? A blast of thorazine strong enough to stagger a lion in the wild? Electro-convulsive shock therapy? All three – and more?

Stone rolled out of bed troubled, but immediately did what he had done for each of the previous eleven mornings. He read the last page of Ezra's little plan to get him through – and out of – hell. He had already made it, but he knew that this was about more than getting through hell. This was about living – and he was going to need God's plan for how to do it – everyday – for as long as he lived. So, he read:

"In view of all this, what can we say? If God is for us, who can be against us? Certainly not God, who did not even keep back his own Son, but offered him for us all! He gave up his Son – will He not also freely give us all things? Who will accuse God's chosen people? God himself declares them not guilty! Who, then, will condemn them? Not Christ Jesus, who died, or rather, who was raised to life and is at the right side of God, pleading with Him for us! Who, then, can separate us from the love of Christ? Can hardship or persecution or

hunger or poverty or danger or death? . . . No, in all these things we have complete victory through him who loved us!"[51]

And Hallelujah Livingstone was hit with a mighty wave of peace and a soothing revelation that threw him backwards onto his psych ward bed, belly-laughing and shouting out loud, "Ezra Eliot Loleko – locked in a state bughouse, for who knows how long – has complete victory! Complete victory! Through him who loved us – in spite of our wicked ways! And Stone laughed and cackled and boomed the very last words of Ezra's Holy Spirit-inspired Plan:

"For I am certain that nothing can separate us from his love: neither death nor life, neither angels nor other heavenly rulers or powers, neither the world above nor the world below – there is nothing in all creation that will ever be able to separate us from the love of God which is ours through Christ Jesus our Lord."[52]

And Hallelujah Livingstone roared out a howling, country-punk, coyote wail, *"You can stand me up . . . at the GATES of HELL . . . but I WON'T . . . BACK . . . DOWN!"*[53]

And Hallelujah Livingstone smiled.

No hell could hold him.

No hell could take his joy.

———————————————— ⑉ ————————————————

Thanks for reading Ezra's plan. Give it to a friend and discuss it with him or her like Ezra discussed it with Hallelujah. You will encourage your friend and reinforce the plan in your own spirit. And (I'll be crassly honest) you will help me sell a couple of books to people who are going through hell. Everybody does – sooner or later – probably more than once. And you know the way out. Show them the way out!

Richard Jarzynka

END NOTES

1. Matthew 6: 7a
2. Matthew 6: 7-8
3. Matthew 6: 7-8
4. Matthew 6: 7a
5. Matthew 5:1-2
6. Matthew 5:1a
7. Matthew 5:1b-2
8. Matthew 5:1-2
9. Matthew 5: 1-2
10. Matthew 5: 1b
11. Matthew 5:3-4
12. Psalm 32: 10a
13. Psalm 32: 10b
14. Psalm 32: 10b
15. Jonah 2: 2b, 3a, 4a, 6b
16. Jonah 2: 3a, 6b, 2b
17. Jonah 2: 2b-3
18. Jonah 2: 4
19. Jonah 2: 5-6a
20. Jonah 2: 6b-7
21. Jonah 2: 3b, 3a, 6b
22. Jonah 2: 6b
23. Jonah 2: 6b-7a
24. Psalm 32: 1-5
25. Psalm 32: 8-9
26. Psalm 32: 10-11

27. Psalm 142: 1-3
28. Psalm 142: 1a
29. Psalm 142: 1b-2
30. Psalm 142: 1a
31. Psalm 142: 1b-2
32. Newton, John (1725-1807) "Amazing Grace." (1779).
33. Amazing Grace
34. John 14: 1-7
35. McFerrin, Bobby. (1950 -), "Don't Worry, Be Happy" 1988, Manhattan
36. John 14: 1a
37. John 14: 1a
38. John 14: 1b
39. John 14: 3b
40. Psalm 23: 1-6
41. Luke 10: 42-43
42. 1 Thessalonians 4: 13-18
43. Philippians 4: 4a
44. Philippians 4: 4b
45. Philippians 4: 5a
46. Philippians 4: 5b – 6a
47. Philippians 4: 6-7a
48. Philippians 4: 7
49. Philippians 4: 8-9
50. Acts 4: 33-37
51. Romans 8: 31-35, 37
52. Romans 8: 38-39
53. Petty, Tom. (1950 -). "I Won't Back Down." From the Album "Full Moon Fever." 1989, MCA Records.

Printed in the United States
By Bookmasters